sugar & spite
a sweetwater novella

dana isaly

Cover Design by Cady at Cruel Ink Editing & Design

Formatting by Dana Isaly

Editing by Sandra at One Love Editing

theme song

Wondering Why by The Red Clay Strays

prologue

. . .

Kara

ONE YEAR AGO...

Staring at all of the equipment and supplies I shoved into the back of my minivan, I realize this was a really, really stupid idea. And, honestly, I can just add it to all of the stupid ideas I've made lately. Like dropping out of college to pursue my dream of owning my own coffee shop. And moving to a small town in the middle of freaking nowhere because it was where the dart landed that I threw at a map. Like leaving behind all of my friends and family to move here because I'm not one to go back on my word.

Listen, when the person you think you're going to spend the rest of your life with cheats on you, it makes you do some crazy shit.

So instead of staring at it like I'll miraculously develop telekinesis, I grab as much as I can and head back to the table and tent I claimed on Main Street. Today is Sweet-

1

water Saturday's. Every second Saturday of the month, the town of Sweetwater Springs puts on an event for anyone who makes and sells things. Small businesses, artists, jewelry makers, and the like rent a table and sell their goods. Agatha, my landlord, told me when I signed the lease that I should make my debut there. And here I am.

I got here ridiculously early so that I could claim a table and start setting up before other people started trickling in. The thought of being the new person in town and showing up to this event when everyone else is already here... no, thank you. My anxiety says that's a hard pass.

My arms are screaming as I clamor through the back street, down the block, and then out into the main drag of downtown. The tent I chose is right in front of my new shop and at the forefront of the festival. It's perfect. I can take all of my stuff right into the empty shop after the event is over, and it helps that I can tell everyone I'll be open within a week, right behind where I'll be sitting.

But when I make it back to my tent, my cooler that I used to hold my place has moved. It's now sitting on the second table, and there's a large, lumberjack-looking man sitting with his feet up in front of my shop. At *my* table.

"Excuse me?" I ask as I get closer.

"Oh, need a hand?" He's all smiles as he rushes out of his chair and charges toward me. Christ, he's huge. He towers more than a foot over me, and between his biceps and the broad chest, I'm a little intimidated. His green eyes sparkle behind his glasses.

"Uh..." I stammer and can't seem to get my words out. He grabs a few things out of my arms and then stands there and looks at me. His eyes are friendly and crinkled on the sides as he just continues to smile at my awkwardness.

"Thank you," I finally spit out. "But I was supposed to be at that table." I nod in the direction of where he was sitting with my head.

His eyebrows knit together as he looks over at the table and then back to me, and then back to the table again.

"I had my cooler there." I point with my elbow. "And now it's over there." Another point with my elbow.

"Well, I didn't touch your stuff, but there was nothing here when I showed up." He walks over to the second table and sets down the bags he took from me before returning to take the rest. His chivalry is annoying me.

"So I suppose it just blew over to the other table? A strong gust of wind made it and the fifty pounds of ice inside just take flight?"

He thinks I'm being funny. His eyes are light with humor as they meet my own, very serious ones. I'm not making a good impression. I know I shouldn't make a scene. Just go to the second table and shut up already. But I really wanted this table. I wanted to be right in front of my new shop. I wanted to decorate it with pretty lettering and designs so that people would be drawn over to it and to my business.

I needed that table, dammit.

"Grady," he announces, shoving his hand in my direction. "What's your name, Tink? Don't think I've seen you around."

"Tink?"

3

"Yeah. Small, grumpy, a little feisty."

"Oh! Kara!" I turn around to see a short, graying woman jogging in our direction. "It's Agatha. How lovely to meet you finally!"

"Kara," Grady says in his smooth voice behind me. "You're the new girl."

"Something like that," I say over my shoulder.

"I see you've met Grady." Agatha wraps me up in a hug and then blushes as she does the same to Grady. "Lovely that you're both here. Kara, darling, so sorry to have moved your stuff. But the winner of the prior year's Valentine's Day competition wins the lead table the following year. A little perk."

Her nose scrunches as she smiles and moves over to look at all my things Grady sat on the tables.

"See?" Grady says with another charming smile as he bumps my shoulder. "Told you I didn't touch your stuff."

I ignore him.

"Agatha, I was hoping to have the table in front of my future shop." I follow her around the tables. "I wanted to decorate the windows a bit and direct people that could be future customers."

"Oh, don't be silly, dear." She grabs my gloved hand with her very cold, bare one. "You can definitely still do those things! You're not far away at all. Now." Her voice becomes all business as she tugs out a clipboard from a huge bag on her shoulder. "I'll write you in here, and hopefully, you and Grady can become good friends! He owns a bakery right across the road there. You could send each other customers!"

She looks hopeful, but as I look across the street, all I can see is a gaudy pink storefront that needs some serious updating. The hand-painted letters are starting to chip off and smear in places. The pink is more of a Pepto pink instead of a soft, welcoming sort of color. It's very… strange for the lumberjack to my right.

And it's in complete contrast to what I plan to do with my own business. I have plans to paint everything dark and neutral, with plenty of live plants and leather couches to warm up the cold tile floor that came with the place.

We honestly couldn't be more different.

"Anyway, I'm off. I have a lot to do and not a lot of time to do it! Vendors will start pouring in with questions. Just give me a shout if either of you need anything. And Kara," she says, touching my hand again, "I am so very happy to welcome you to our little town."

With a squeeze of my hand and a soft smile, Agatha disappears.

"Wouldn't have pegged you for a pink man." I chance a glance in his direction and find he's still watching me, his huge arms folded over his chest. The color of his eyes is almost off-putting they're so green.

"I'm happy to trade tables with you. My goodies will draw a crowd no matter where my ass is parked." His eyebrows wag as if he expects me to laugh at his joke.

"No." I take a deep breath and try to get my attitude under control. "It's fine. Like she said, I'm not *that* far away from my storefront. I'll make it work."

"Need help carrying the rest of your stuff?"

"God, you're helpful to a fault, aren't you?" Even I

know that I'm being unnecessarily bitchy, but I'm tired and anxious, and Grady is like a big red target, perfect for taking out all my frustrations. "I've got it. Just focus on your own table, okay? It's looking a little sad."

"Aye, aye," he says with a mock salute and a wink. "Looking forward to working in such close quarters with you, Tink. You're a riot."

I grunt at him and stalk back to my car. So much for getting a good start on my new life.

grady

· · ·

"You sure do watch her a lot." Agatha's voice brings me out of my daydreams and snaps me right back into reality.

"I don't." The spot I've been obsessively polishing on the countertop says otherwise.

"Mhm," she hums as she gives me her signature Agatha grin. The one all kind, experienced, graying women have after their decades of experience. I'm not a fan of it, if I'm honest. "How's business?"

"Great, actually." Finally, a comfortable topic. "Tell you the truth, that gloomy little coffee shop over there has a lot to do with it."

"Oh?" Her eyebrow raises, and she leans forward onto the pickup counter. It's mid-afternoon, the slowest time of the day. No one is in the shop, so Agatha always comes around to gossip.

"Yeah." I toss the rag over my shoulder and awkwardly lean down to match her stance. "She's kicked my ass into gear. All those fancy decorations and fresh paint. Made me feel like this old place needed a facelift as well."

"Has nothing to do with impressing her, then?"

"No." I groan and leave our gossip huddle to bring some fresh banana loaves out of the ovens. "You need to stop shit stirring."

I can hear her scoff behind me, but she doesn't protest. She knows the main reason she's great at her job is because she's in everyone's ear and everyone's shoulder to cry on when they need it. Agatha is a woman of the people, for the people. No one can say no to her when she brings out those baby blues.

She knows she's right about me. I let it slip once when she was in here last summer. I don't know what I was thinking. Sugar rush to the brain. But we were laughing, and she was going on and on about Tink and how she's just been so great for the town. I agreed and then promptly let it slip that it's nice to have a pretty face to look at while I work.

Big mistake. She's latched onto it ever since and won't let go. Jaw locked, foaming at the mouth, waiting for me to get down on one knee and make lots and lots of babies. Agatha is a *sucker* for babies.

But there's no way a girl like that is going to be into a guy like me. I'm too small for her. Not in stature, that's for sure. My six-foot-five *dad bod* is anything but small. But in the way of life. Hell, that girl has been to so many different places it'll make your head spin. She's young, bright, and has her whole damn future ahead of her. She doesn't need some small-town guy from bumfuck nowhere Alabama messing up her plans.

She sure is nice to look at, though. The moment she walked up to me last year with those dark eyes laser focused on me, her cheeks red from the winter wind, and clothes that somehow hugged her body but hid it at the same time…fuck me, I was a goner. She was a breath of fresh — albeit cold — air. Her icy tone and sharp glances in my direction made my dick hard. Especially when it became clear I was the only person in town lucky enough to be on the receiving end of that wrath.

"How's planning going for the festival?"

"Ah, ah," I chide as I slide the loaves onto the cooling racks. "You know I never give any hints."

"The best secret keeper I've ever met," she says, waiting a short moment before turning toward me with a cheeky grin. "Most of the time, anyway."

"Don't you have somewhere to be?"

"I do, actually. Lucky for you." Agatha gathers up her things and shoves the rest of her bagel in her mouth. "Same time tomorrow?"

"Hannah is working tomorrow. I'll be back on the weekend."

She's gone with a sweet smile and a goodbye wave. The sound of the bells chimes loudly as the door swings shut, and I fall right back into watching my friend across the street. It's hard to see with all the fancy lettering she has on her windows, but I can see her standing at the counter, talking to someone. I can always tell it's her because when someone is talking to her, you're her whole world.

She listens to you intently. I watch her interact with her customers or when we happen to bump into each other in the wild. Her dark eyes go soft and eager, and her body language is relaxed and calm. She throws her head back every time she laughs, with a rough cackle bursting forth from her throat like a witch.

It's endearing. But boy, when those eyes land on me… whew. They narrow, her body stiffens, and a slight blush crawls across her pale cheeks. I've caught her looking at me a few times over the past year, and I can't help but hope she likes what she sees. Even though I have a bit of a belly, I work out and stay in shape. I'd like to think if it weren't for how different we are, maybe I'd be her type.

The store phone rings, making me jump. I have *got* to stop staring at her. It's becoming creepy.

"Temptations Bakery, how can I help?"

"You can stop staring at me." Her voice rings clear as a bell through the line. I turn and look out the window, a grin on my face. I see her peering through the window, jaw set and eyebrows tense.

"Well, hi there, Tink." I make a show of waving through my own window. "How's my favorite caffeine pusher?"

"She'd be much better if she didn't catch you staring like a creep every five minutes today!" Her arms flail up in the air. "Stop trying to figure out what I'm doing for the competition. It won't work, Grady."

Fuck, the way she says my name.

"I've won five years in a row. Some cute little girl from the city isn't gonna hurt my chances of getting number six."

Just as I expect, that really gets her riled up. She hates it when I point out she's not from around here.

"I am going to kick your ass, Grady Carter. Up and down Main Street. By the time I'm done with you, you won't know what hit you."

She really knows how to sweet-talk me.

"Can't wait. Now, can I help you with anything else? Some of us have work to do."

"Wouldn't have guessed. You've been cleaning that one spot on the counter all afternoon. Bet it's shinier than a penny."

"You watchin' me, Tink?" If she can't see the smile on my face, she can definitely hear it in my voice. "Like what you see?"

"Bite me, Lurch."

"I'm not *that* tall." I pause for a second. "Or imposing. Or grumpy. Or—"

"Quiet."

"True."

"Goodbye."

The phone clicks, and I laugh as I put it back on the charger. Shit, I think I'm going to marry this girl one day.

kara

. . .

I LOVE the sound a stylus makes on a paper-feel screen protector. It's the most pleasant scratching sound — it just hits a special spot in my brain. I thought maybe I could have a glass of wine, sketch out some ideas for Valentine's Day, and try to relax since I have the next couple of days off. But once I got home, I realized I wanted something a little stronger and maybe a little different than wine.

Special gummy? Yes, please.

My eyes are heavy, and my muscles are relaxed when my friend Mielle lets herself into my house. She became a regular customer at my shop over the last year, and we became fast friends. We regularly invite ourselves over to each other's houses, having dinner dates and TV binge sessions weekly.

"I am cooking," she announces, setting four brown paper bags on the kitchen island.

"Oh, thank god. I'm so hungry." I moan and roll onto

my side, swinging my arm and leg over the back of the couch as I watch her spread the ingredients out on the countertop. "What are you making?"

"Cheese-stuffed tortellini in a mushroom cream sauce."

"You spoil me, Mielle."

"I do. And you are a roasty toasty princess. How many gummies so far?"

I hold up one finger.

"Taking it slow tonight. I just needed to fucking relax." I throw my hands up in the air and roll back onto the cushions.

"Let me guess—"

"Grady," we both say at the same time.

"Why do you let him work his way under your skin?"

"It's impossible not to!" I tap my fist on my forehead. "I caught him *staring* at me today!"

"Staring at you?"

"Yes. Staring. Like, wiping the same spot on his counter, unblinking, *staring*!"

"I'm sure he was just daydreaming."

"He was spying on me, Mielle." I sit up and narrow my eyes on her. "I know it!" I thrust my finger into the air. "He is spying because he knows I'm going to kick ass at this festival."

"I went to school with Grady. I can assure you he is the kindest, most pure-hearted man I've ever met." She pauses her chopping for a second and looks up at me. "It's actually kind of annoying how *good* he is. He was not spying on you. He was looking at you."

"Don't start." The old wood floor creaks under my feet

as I shuffle into the kitchen, desperate to steal little bites as she cooks. I hop up onto one of my stools and pop a mush-room into my mouth.

"I would stop starting if you would quit complaining." She wings her knife around in the air as she speaks, her brown eyes wide and full of expression. "I tell you all the time he is *looking* at you. He likes you. He wants to…" She trails off and wags her eyebrows. "You know."

"He is infuriating. Never happening."

"Never say never, ma petite amie pessimiste."

"Ce n'est pas parce que je porte du noir que je suis pessimiste." *Just because I wear black does not make me a pessimist.*

"Your French is getting better."

She smiles like a proud mama bear. Her family moved here right before Mielle was a freshman in high school. She was taught English growing up, but it is laced pretty heavily with a French accent she never quite lost. I was told when we first met that if I didn't make an effort to learn French, we couldn't be friends. She was joking, of course, but I decided I needed a hobby. My French can be rough, *really* rough. But, hey, it's fun.

"You know, I must say, the best sex I've ever had was when we both couldn't stand each other. It was like all that anger made the passion so much bigger and brighter." With her back to me as she readies the stove, I steal another mushroom.

"Look, don't get me wrong. The guy is attractive. No one can deny that." Mielle agrees with a knowing nod. "But he is so full of himself! And he's constantly trying to one-up me. I paint my windows, he paints his windows. I decorate the outdoor seating, he gives the entire front of his shop a paint job. I start making a coffee of the day, he starts making a pastry of the day to match it."

"That was actually so sweet, though," she coos. "He did it so you could send each other customers!"

I take a deep breath and reach for the bag of gummies. One more can't hurt. I'll eat my body weight in pasta, turn on a movie, and fall into the best sleep of my life once Mielle heads back to her own place. It's exactly what I need to shake this off.

"So, what's your plan, then?" she says after a heavy sigh.

"What do you mean?"

"He embarrassed you last year at the festival — your words, not mine. Because he took your table, ruined your day, and won the price at the end of it. So you want to get him back and win this year. What's your plan?"

The onion and mushrooms mix together in the pan with garlic and butter. My stomach growls painfully. I don't think I'm going to make it. Chips. I need some chips. And dip. Definitely going to get that dip out of the fridge.

"Stop that." She slaps my hand as I reach across to the basket where the Doritos are just crying out for me. "You'll ruin your appetite. Sit down. Tell me your ideas."

"Well," I say, laughing humorlessly. "I don't really have one."

"You do not have a plan?"

I shake my head.

"Not a clue?"

"Nope." Another shake.

"And yet you're trash-talking him daily. To his face." Her lips roll in, and she tries her best not to laugh. But she can't help it, and I don't blame her.

I lay my forehead down on the cool granite.

"I am all bark and no bite."

"You are not the Valentine's Day type, I'm afraid."

Her words are harsh, but her tone is loving. She's right, though. I'm not. I'm not into all this pink and red, lovey-dovey crap. The expensive flowers and disgusting choco-lates. The idea that if your partner dotes on you for one day out of the year, it's an excuse for them to fuck off the other 364 days. Treat me special every day we are together. You shouldn't need a holiday to go on a date or get a compliment.

Bah fucking humbug.

"But Grady, on the other hand?" She grins as she stirs. "That man is all sunshine and rainbows. Has been as long as I've known him. Maybe just take your Halloween win and call it a day?"

I could. I really could. And I should. Autumn is my season, and Halloween is my holiday. I go all out every year, and I knew I could really show out with the decora-tions and recipes. It was hardly a contest. After everyone tasted my special salted caramel, green apple cider slushies, it was over. Everyone just kept coming back for more, and it was over for Grady.

At the end of the afternoon, I looked up to rub it in his face, only to find him staring at me again with that stupid, sweet smile on his face.

"Congratulations," he said as he walked over, arm outstretched to shake my hand. "You deserved that. That shit was good."

Before I could protest, he wrapped my hand up in his own, his grip strong and sure. And he didn't stop there. No, no, He tugged me into a hug that crushed me up against his chest. His very broad, very manly chest that smelled of maple sugar candy and pine. It was the strangest combination, and yet I found myself breathing him in for just a second too long.

Afterward, I didn't say a word. Just walked away like nothing had happened. Went into my shop and didn't dare leave until he was gone. I still can't figure out why he keeps smiling at me, pushing my buttons, and just being a freaking menace. It drives me insane.

"Here. Eat." Mielle shoves a plate filled with delicious-smelling, cheesy pasta under my nose.

How long have I been daydreaming?

"A while."

"I said that out loud?" I ask around a mouthful.

"You did." She laughs, and I can't help but think it sounds like wind chimes. Woof, that second gummy may not have been a good idea. "Now, let's watch some trashy reality TV until you can't stay awake any longer."

kara

. . .

THE DOOR to the coffee shop swings open, and the brass bells I hung from the doorknob jangle loudly as Mielle sweeps in. Her cheeks are bright pink from the cold wind, and her eyes are lit up with something I don't quite like.

"Why do you look like you're up to something?"

"Oh, I'm not," she answers, taking a seat at the small bar in front of me. "But Agatha sure is."

"What do you mean?"

"Check your email."

A sense of dread sweeps through my stomach, and I almost don't want to log in and check. God knows what Agatha has done now. She means well, but my goodness, she loves to meddle, and she's had it out for me and Grady ever since that first day.

The email at the top of the list has a subject line in all caps: URGENT INFO FOR UPCOMING EVENT.

I let out a long sigh, and Mielle just kicks her legs and giggles.

"Happy season of love, everyone!

I'm writing this email to thank you all for the overwhelming support we've had for this upcoming Valentine's Day Sweet Treat competition. We have had so many vendors apply that we've run out of street space!

So instead of turning people away or going through all the paperwork the city requires to extend the event at the last minute, myself and the other sponsors have decided we should change it up a little!"

Fuck. Fuck. Fuck.

"This year, all of you will be paired up with someone. You'll have to work together over the next two weeks to come up with something that fits BOTH of your personalities and businesses! We think this is a great way to bring the community together and build stronger bonds between all vendors. We can't wait to see what you all come up with!

You'll find a list of names below, including the business name and contact information so that you can get started. We tried to pair everyone up with who we thought would be complementary to your current business practice. As always, if you have any issues or questions/concerns, please reach out! Send me an email, give me a call, or tackle me in the street. Hah!

Happy Valentine's Day — and may the best businesses win!"

Okay, so they paired us up. No biggie. She said they put us with people who complement our styles and such, so surely I've been partnered with literally anyone except Grady. We couldn't be more different. There is no way we would be matched.

I start scrolling, glancing up at Mielle only to see her watching me intently…smirking. Ugh, the dread in my stomach is starting to make me feel sick. The names are in alphabetical order, and I don't see Grady's name yet. So I scroll past the G's until I get to where I know I'll be.

And there it is.

Kara Gallant – Roasted with Grady Carter — Temptations Bakery

"I can tell by the look on your face you've just read the email." Grady walks up to both of us. I didn't even hear the bells announce his arrival over the pounding in my ears.

"I personally think you two are going to be great." Mielle smiles up at him from where she sits, her chin resting in the palm of her hand. She looks ornery as hell. If I didn't love her so much, I might slap her.

"Between you and me," he whispers as if I'm not standing right here, "I think so, too." He winks at her and then trains those piercing green eyes on me.

God, why does he have to be so…annoying.

"It'll be okay, Tink. It's only two weeks. And then we can go back to hating each other."

"Whatever." I roll my eyes. "How Agatha ever thought we would mesh well together, I don't know. Your shop literally looks like a Pepto bottle threw up all over it. And I haven't worn the color pink since I was five."

"Well, it is Valentine's Day," he says, not bothering to

bite back the grin on his face. "Maybe she thought you needed a little pink in your life."

"I guess we should get to work. I'll be honest," I say with a sigh. "I haven't really had any ideas on what to do. So I'm afraid you may have been stuck with a dud for a partner."

"Don't worry, Tink. I'll pick up the slack." He starts walking back toward the door. "I'll pick you up at closing."

"Wait!" He turns around. "Why?"

"Because we need to get started. I'm not about to lose my first Valentine's Day competition. I've won six years in a row, and you aren't gonna ruin that." He smiles. "See you at six."

A burst of cold air comes in as he leaves, and I can't help but just stare after him. No one should be allowed to look that goddamn good. It infuriates me.

"You look at him like you want to eat him up."

"I do not!" I whip my head in Mielle's direction immediately.

"You're always talking about how he's staring at you, but girl…" She fans herself. "You have the hots for Grady."

"Wrong."

"I mean, you could do a whole lot worse." She pushes on like she didn't even hear me. "He's got that whole big and tall lumberjack thing going for him. Pretty sure he could lift a car with those biceps. Sure, he has a little bit of a tummy on him, but I happen to think dad bods are hot."

"Maybe you should date him, then." I give her a look, begging her to shut up.

"Nah, he is head over heels for you. I don't want to get in the way of your happily ever after." She sighs and looks wistfully out of the front windows. They're currently decorated with dark reds and warm neutrals. Coffee beans and bloody hearts. "Bet he could throw you around the bedroom."

"Okay!" I throw my hands up in the air. "You're done."

Mielle laughs, filling the otherwise empty coffee shop with humor.

"I'm just sayin'. I heard some seriously raunchy rumors in high school."

I raise an eyebrow, and she lifts her hands up in front of her face, spreading them farther and farther apart until we both dissolve into a fit of giggles.

"There's no way."

She shrugs. "He's a big guy. Wouldn't surprise me if they were true."

That sends my mind spiraling into places I haven't let it go in the entire year I've been here. Within the first week I moved here, I was having a little private fun time, and his face popped up in my brain without my permission just as I was about to...finish. Ever since, I've stayed as far away from Grady Carter as I could, refusing to let myself get involved.

I'm willingly celibate after having been burned far too many times by love and sex. It's messy, and it always leads to heartbreak. This was supposed to be my fresh start, a way to get on with my life after my ex-fiancé cheated on me. This town was how I was going to heal.

And I have. Mostly because I've run in the opposite

direction of Grady Carter every chance I get. But now I don't have that option. We're stuck together. I know Agatha, and she put us together for a reason. There's no way she'd let me drop out or request to change partners. And honestly, I'd feel bad.

Sure, Grady gets on my last fucking nerve almost daily. But he's never actually done anything horrible to me. He's nothing but sickeningly nice. I can put up with him for two weeks, and heck, maybe we'll win. I wouldn't mind a little redemption, even if I do have to share it with Mr. Lumberjack across the road.

There are worse things in life.

I just have to hope my willpower can survive the next two weeks.

kara

. . .

IT'S RAINING, so I'm standing under the awning of my shop, waiting for Grady to pick me up. The shop was dead because of the rain and cold, so I ended up closing a little early. It was tempting, the idea of running home to turn off my phone and hide under the covers. But I'm pretty sure Grady would hunt me down. And there's no getting out of this. We have to get this done because forfeiting is not an option for me.

His truck pulls up within a few minutes, and he jumps out to run around the hood. He's wearing a dark blue Carhartt with the hood up, covering his messy blond hair, but rain is still leaving drops on his glasses. His smile is wide as he jogs through the puddles. Ever the gentleman, even in the rain, he opens the passenger-side door and gestures me over.

"Hop in, Tink."

"You didn't have to open the door for me," I grumble

as I stalk past him quickly. The truck is an old, beat-up, boxy thing that was probably popular thirty years ago. I'd like to think I'm not one to judge a book by its cover, but if this cold ends up freezing this rain, I don't think this is a car I want to be in.

"Wanted to," he says before closing the door and running back around to his side. He climbs in with that damn smile still plastered on his face. His cheeks are a bit red from the chill in the air, and it looks incredibly endearing. Which just makes me mad.

"I have a feeling this might freeze." He leans forward and squints out the windshield. "Supposed to get cold tonight."

"I assume you can have me home before that happens?" I ask as we take off down Main.

"I'll get you home before you turn into a pumpkin, Tink. Don't worry."

"I'm just slightly concerned about this thing." I lean forward and tap the dashboard.

He gasps and clutches his chest. "Don't you talk bad about Betsy. She's gotten me through rain, sleet, and snow. This old gal knows what she's doing."

I raise my eyebrows but don't say another word, just hold my hands up and sit back in my seat. The town passes us by as we make our way out to his house. I'm not sure exactly where he lives, even though this is a small town and everyone knows everything about everyone, but I have heard that he's out in the countryside. And that, yet again, doesn't make me feel any better about being out in this weather. I know Alabama has a bad track record for taking care of their roads in cold weather.

"Guess I should've asked if you like dogs?" His voice startles me out of my thoughts. It's been a pretty quiet ride, but as we turn into what I assume is his gravel driveway, I realize I've been zoned out for a while.

"Love dogs."

His house comes into view, and it's gorgeous. Definitely not as I was expecting. Although I'm a decent bit younger than him, so every guy I've dated hasn't been as established in their career. I guess that makes a difference because damn, this place is gorgeous. He's painted it a dark navy, and there's a wraparound porch with ceiling fans that must be amazing in the southern summers.

"Good," he says as we pull into the garage. "Because Hank is going to love all over you. He loves visitors."

The garage door closes behind us, and I suddenly feel very claustrophobic. I am very, very alone with this man... in his house.

"Oh, and if you wouldn't mind, could you take your shoes off? Hank decided to run in the mud yesterday and then sneak past me through the door. So I was mopping the floors all night. I'm hoping to keep them clean for longer than a day."

"You aren't going to kill me, right?" He opens the door, and I peek around him, getting a glimpse of what looks like a normal mudroom. I don't know what I'm looking for, but all I see is wood flooring and cream walls. Nothing that screams "I have a dungeon in my basement."

"If I waited this long to lure you into my home just to

kill you," he says as he kicks off his boots, "that would make me a very, very patient serial killer."

"Mhm," I hum, kicking off my own boots and shrugging off my coat. He takes it for me and hangs it on a rack behind the door. "I guess at this point, it's too late to turn back."

"Just get your cute butt inside, Tink. Hank is going to be chomping at the bit to meet you."

grady

. . .

HAVING her in my truck cab, her spice-and-coffee scent wrapping around me, was one of the most difficult things I've ever had to endure. She doesn't realize how head over heels I am for her scorned looks and angry pouts. I wanted nothing more than to reach out and touch her, hold her hand, run the pad of my thumb over the soft skin of her knuckles.

And if I thought that was hard to resist, having her in my home is a whole different ball game. Hank has been let out of the sunroom, where I keep him when I'm gone, and he's loving the crap out of her. I'm glad she likes dogs and doesn't seem to be scared of big ones because Hank is all over her.

This would be easy to get used to, her in this house, comfortable and laughing.

"I've never seen a Dobie with floppy ears!" she

exclaims, the happiest I've seen her when in my presence. "He's the cutest fucking thing I've ever seen."

I laugh at her casual f-bomb.

"Got him when he was a puppy from some backyard breeder that hadn't done the cropping yet. And I'm not one for doing painful things unnecessarily."

I open the fridge and look at the meal I had planned for myself for tonight. I'm a little embarrassed it isn't something fancier. But I know it's good, and if she tries it, I'll convert her to Southern cooking soon enough.

"You okay with meatloaf and scalloped potatoes?" She walks over to inspect everything as I sit the glass casserole dishes down on the counter and tug off the aluminum foil. "Nothing fancy, but it's an easy meal to put together the night before."

"I love meatloaf, actually." Her eyes look at me suspiciously, like I've done this on purpose. "What's scalloped potatoes, though?"

"You've never had—?" I sigh. "My god, woman. They're just cheesy potatoes, and they're delicious. Right, Hank?"

He gives me a roo and a nudge with his nose in agreement.

"I like cheese, and I like potatoes." She gives me a quick, genuine smile before turning on her heel and walking away, and I feel my heart skip a beat. What I wouldn't give to see her look at me like that all the time. "You have a really nice house."

"Thank you." The oven beeps as I turn it on and then slide both dishes inside. "Worked hard for it."

"I'm kind of surprised, actually." Her hands are on her hips as she surveys the pictures on the walls and the furniture in the living room. "I figured it would be a bachelor pad, with beer posters and open chip bags laying around."

"Kara, I'm thirty, not twenty-one. I realized you're young and used to frat boys, but give me some credit."

The second the words are out of my mouth, I regret them. Her playful smile drops, and her eyes go angry again. Always so angry. She seems too small to carry all of that. She's a wisp of a thing, her dark hair hitting just at her slender shoulders. The rest of her body always seems to be covered with layers of soft clothing, even in the summer. Sometimes, though, she takes a little risk and wears shorts. The first time I saw her thighs last summer, I thought I was going to lose my damn mind.

"You're right." Her voice cuts through my thoughts.

Well, damn. Maybe she's coming around to me.

"I think we should start over." Kara clears her throat and walks around the island and into my space. That damned warm scent of hers wraps around me all over again. "Hi, I'm Kara."

I look down at her hand, outstretched toward me, and I can feel the sparks of excitement in my belly. It's just a hand, but it represents so much more.

"Hi, Kara." I take her hand in my own, dwarfing it. "Grady."

I'm probably imagining it, but I swear I see the slightest pink tinge on her cheeks.

"Nice to meet you, Grady." Too soon, her hand is being taken from my own. "Now that we're on better terms, I have something to admit."

My eyebrow cocks up towards my hairline.

I'm in love with you, too, I think to myself.

"I have literally no clue what I want to do for this competition."

I slowly blink at her.

"You?" I ask, my voice incredulous. "The woman who always has a game plan? The woman who shows up every Sweetwater Saturday ready to kick my ass? That woman?"

She laughs again, and I wish I could bottle it up. It's now my mission to make her laugh as much as possible. I want to hear that wind chime laughter every day for the rest of my life. Christ, I'm in deep for this woman. This woman who, before ten seconds ago, wanted nothing to do with me. Hated me, in fact. At least, I thought she did. But maybe now that we've started over, I have some semblance of a chance.

"Valentine's Day is not my favorite holiday. I know you'd never guess by looking at me." She gestures down to her all-dark ensemble. "But I've just never been a fan. I think growing up the ugly duckling in school kind of ruined any joy Valentine's might bring."

"Alright, well, that just won't do." I rummage around in my cabinets, looking for something I know I have stashed. I'm not a big drinker. Honestly, the last time I had a drink was almost a year ago when she walked into town. I came straight home and took three shots of the only alcohol I keep in my house.

I went through a time where work was so stressful I was having a glass or two every night after work. Then I'd wake up feeling like shit. Alcohol was never a problem for me growing up, but I realized that I was becoming far too dependent on it when I had a bad day. So I pretty much stopped drinking altogether three or so years ago. Ever since then, if there's a little edge I need to take off, I eat a little edible instead. No hangover, less dependence, and a way better pick-me-up.

"What are you doing?"

"Take a seat." I gesture over toward the living room as I finally find the bottle of whiskey that got pushed to the back of my spices cabinet. "You're going to have a shot, loosen up a bit, and get the ideas flowing."

"We are *not* drinking." I follow her into the living room and sit closer than I would've dared if this happened yesterday. I don't think I can help myself. Seeing her curl up on my couch, her legs folded under her and a pillow on her lap, she looks so right here.

"I'm not," I tell her, pouring a finger of scotch into a thick clear glass. "But you are."

My arm is extended, holding the amber liquid between us. She eyes it.

"Not to be a Debbie Downer, but...I don't really drink. I've never been able to stand the taste." This time, I know I'm not seeing things when her face blushes. It even crawls down her neck, and I immediately feel bad for putting her on the spot. That's what I get for just assuming everyone drinks. "I'm more of an edible girlie."

A big grin breaks out across my face until my cheeks hurt. She stares at me like I've grown another head.

"What?" she asks, leaning back into the couch and away from me.

"A woman after my own heart," I say, clutching my chest.

"You're still not partaking," she says, shaking her little finger back and forth.

"Wouldn't dream of it, Tink. I have precious cargo to get home later and shitty weather conditions." I wink at her before going off in search of gummies. "But that doesn't mean you can't."

kara

. . .

"YOU'RE GOING to sit there and tell me that nothing happened?"

Mielle is sitting at the counter while I put together the coffee that I think is going to be the winner. Grady and I discussed flavors last night, and we — well, I — struggled to see his vision of an explosion of pinks and reds. I finally convinced him to let me try some ideas first since this competition is supposed to highlight both of our styles. Once I get mine nailed down, we can build off that. And I conceded to let him veto anything he deems to dark.

"Nothing happened," I reiterate as I roll the vintage depression glass in marshmallow fluff. "He made dinner, I cuddled with his dog, and we discussed the competition. After that, he drove me home."

She sighs and hangs her head in her hands. So disappointed. I know she wants something to happen between Grady and me, but I just don't see it working. We've been at each other's throats for a year, barely able to stand each other's presence.

"Getting laid wouldn't be the end of the world, you know."

She says it loud enough to make me nervous that someone else heard, and I look around frantically, only to find the few people in the shop are too involved in their phones to notice.

"You're loud," I tell her, pointing an accusing finger in her direction. "And I know it wouldn't, but Mielle, it's not like that. I can barely stand the guy. And god knows he can barely stand me."

"Are you fucking blind?"

I widen my eyes, trying to give her the hint to lower her voice.

"You're so dramatic." I roll my eyes and go through the motions of making the coffee, adding ice and the syrups I think will work well together. "We decided to start over last night and try to be friends. But he's still an annoying little golden retriever, not someone I want to...you know."

Lies, lies, lies. All of it lies. Not the annoying part. I do find his constant optimism to be like nails on a chalkboard. But everything else? I inwardly groan. The man is fine, and the more Mielle mentions it, the more I start daydreaming about it. The only reason I've made it through this past year as a single woman is to put him out of my mind as much as possible. To ignore him as much as possible. To hate him.

"Here." I slide my latest concoction across the counter and sprinkle some pink- and red-dyed sugar on top of the foam. In the competition, I'd have it in a cute little design, but for now, this works. "Tell me what you think."

"Tell me what it is first." She looks at it over her turned-up nose, sniffing as she leans forward. Mielle also has an aversion to all things pink. I like to think it's just another sign that we were meant to be besties.

"Dark chocolate mocha with an extra shot and raspberry and cane sugar syrup to sweeten it up a bit. Marshmallow fluff on the rim. Pink stuff is just colored sugar."

"Sounds like I will be developing diabetes with one sip."

"Just try it," I say, rolling my eyes and laughing.

Her face contorts as she takes a sip.

"Non, pas bon." She slides it back across the counter. "Too bitter."

I groan and take a sip as well. She's right, it is on the bitter side.

"Do it with white chocolate. And then the raspberry syrup can color it to a pretty pink color."

"I was trying to avoid that," I tell her, my grumpiness leaking into my voice. "It's supposed to represent both of us, remember?"

"Maybe you could make the pink, sweet item, and Grady could make something that's more your vibe. Switch it up, show that you're really willing to work together."

I don't hate that idea. It could snag us the win if we do it right. I think most people, if not all, will combine their efforts into one mishmashed piece, or they'll make things that complement each other. But I don't think anyone would switch up their styles like that. It's hard when you're set in your ways with a certain aesthetic to suddenly switch it up. Especially when you've been partnered up with someone who is the exact opposite of you.

"I'll ask him. See if he can even come up with something in my range."

Mielle snorts. "You're so haughty."

My mouth drops. "Excuse me?"

"You are!" she says through laughter. "Don't get me wrong, it's very French of you, and I love it. I love you. But you are a bit proud, ma chérie."

"Ugh!" I let my head fall into my hands. "I don't mean to be. I think my walls are just up."

"You are very defensive. You should lower those walls."

"Okay, thank you, Mielle." I give her a look. "You got your point across."

She holds up her hands, a playful look crossing her face.

"Although," she continues, "maybe you should keep doing what you're doing. It seemed to work on Grady."

"Will you knock it off with the Grady stuff?"

"Jamais!" *Never!*

"Tu as de la chance que je t'aime." *You're lucky I love you.*

I look out of my front window and watch my nemesis and partner across the street. The view hasn't changed much over the past year. Sure, he gave the place a face lift with a new, calmer shade of pink. But other than that, it has remained a constant. And even though he isn't my favorite person and pink isn't my favorite color, the sight of that little bakery has become a comfort.

I'm starting to wonder if maybe I went too hard on my hatred for him. It was just a gut reaction. My anxiety was already heightened, and then to have him throw me off on my first day in town…my mind just shut down toward him. I couldn't look at him without remembering how I felt that day, how embarrassed I was for really no reason. But I didn't want to admit that.

But now I'm wondering if I've missed out on something there. He's been nothing but nice, even though I've given him the cold shoulder for an entire year. Like he can sense I'm looking at him, he turns toward the window, a sheet pan filled with some sort of pastries in his hand, and makes a show of waving in my direction.

Before I know it, I'm laughing and waving back.

"Look at that," Mielle whispers. I ignore her. "The walls are crumbling."

kara

. . .

I'VE SPENT every night this past week at Grady's house, hanging out with him and Hank while we try different recipes and search Pinterest for cute ideas we could maybe mesh together. Every day after work, he picks me up and then cooks me dinner before driving me home at a respectable hour.

It's been...fun. I never thought I'd say those words. I was determined for almost a year to stay as far away from Grady Carter as I could, and now, I'm in his house every day. The food is amazing, the dog cuddles are top-tier, and his house is actually the coziest. Hank lies on top of me now as I stroke his floppy ears, his big toe beans smelling like the freshest bag of Fritos. Today, Grady started a fire for us because there's a cold front coming in from the north that has the temperature dropping far below what Alabama seems to be used to.

"I'll have to take you back a bit earlier tonight." Grady

walks into the living room, two plates filled with steak, mashed potatoes, and cornbread. He shoos Hank off my lap and hands me one of the heavy plates. "I'm afraid the county won't get out here and salt the roads before conditions start to deteriorate."

"Okay, well, I played around with some stuff at work today." I chew a bite of steak. Holy shit, this man is a good cook. I haven't had a single meal that I didn't like. Between him and Mielle, I may never have to cook again. "I've been playing with our idea of a white-chocolate raspberry coffee. I made a few today and tested them on the customers, decorated the tops differently each time to kind of get a feel as to what looks the best."

I dig my phone out of my back pocket and open up my pictures.

"These are the five different designs." He takes my phone. "Just flip to the right. I want to know what your favorite is before I tell you mine."

Out of the corner of my eye, I watch as he thumbs through them a few times. By the time he's done, my plate is half-gone. Jeans may have been a mistake. I can already feel the need to unbutton.

"This one is my favorite. But it doesn't seem to fit your aesthetic. It's far too pink for your liking."

He gives me back my phone, the drink that was also my favorite showing on the screen. I rolled the rim of the coffee cup in marshmallow and then in pink and red sugar. On top of the coffee foam, I created a stencil that allowed me to put the same pink and red sugar in the shape of hearts. I took Mielle's advice and did a white chocolate instead, creating a swirl of white, pink, and red throughout the whole thing.

It's simple, but everyone told me it looks the most festive, and god knows it's going to have to look festive to match what Grady comes up with.

"Why're you smiling like that?" he asks, bringing me back to the moment.

"It's just my favorite as well," I tell him. "And I was thinking it's the most festive, which is something I'll need to make sure it matches what you're doing. The King of Pink."

He looks at me for a second, his teeth biting the inside of his lips before he can't hold it back any longer. A burst of laughter flies out of him, startling Hank, who had taken up residence next to the fire. Grady's face turns red, and I'm so lost.

"Okay, you're looking insane. What did I say?"

It takes him a moment to calm down enough to speak. I can even see a few stray tears in the corners of his eyes.

"King of Pink." His voice is still strained, and it takes a minute before it sinks in.

"Get your mind out of the gutter!" I roll my eyes. "I was actually thinking…well, actually, Mielle had this idea. Now that I've got my design and taste down, maybe you should do something that fits into my aesthetic a bit more? Like we could swap and show us working together like that?"

We've been holding off on thinking about his design and stuff until I could get mine nailed down. He said it would help him decide what to do if I could get mine done first.

"I actually love that idea," he says, sitting his plate off to the side. "So I just need to come up with something dark and moody. Maybe something with walls around it."

I can't help but roll my eyes.

"I think I've made some great strides in the moody department this past week, thank you very much."

"You know, we've never discussed why you decided to move here. It seems like a very random, very small town to choose."

I shrug. "Bad breakup. I always wanted to start a coffee shop. I actually had plans to rent this cute little place my ex found in my hometown, but once everything happened with him, I didn't want to be there anymore. Not because I didn't want to be around him, per se. Mainly just because it felt like everywhere I went, there were memories. And I wanted to start my business baby in a place that didn't have negative things attached to it."

The entire time I talk, Grady is focused on me, his eyes never leaving my face. He's the best listener I think I've ever met outside of Mielle. He really gives me his full attention, whether I'm shit talking or saying something serious. It makes you feel like you're the only person in the room.

"I think that's really brave."

The statement catches me off guard. I guess I never looked at it like that.

"Thank you." I give him a small smile, the air in the room changing as the conversation has turned to something more serious. "I don't think I've ever thought of myself as being brave."

"You left your boyfriend. You left the safety of your family and friends. You completely started over in a new town where you didn't know a single soul. And not only all of that, but you made your business a success." He reaches over, closing the small gap between us, and squeezes my hand. Suddenly, there's an ache in the back of my throat. "I don't think I've seen you have a single slow day at that place. You're impressive."

"You'd know," I tease, trying to diffuse this new tension he's created. "You're always watching, aren't you? My little stalker."

"Little?" His eyebrows shoot up. "This coming from the person that has called me Lurch for an entire year?"

"If the shoe fits." I shrug and smile at him.

"I'm serious, though, Kara." His hand is still on mine, his thumb creating patterns on my knuckles. "You're impressive. You're the strongest woman I think I've come across."

"I'm starting to think you might have a crush on me, Lurch."

The words come out before I can stop them. I realize my mistake the second they escape my mouth, but there's no taking it back now. Instead of laughing it off, like I hope he does, he just stares at me with a slight smile. I swear he's just trying to make me uncomfortable. He gives my hand one more squeeze, and I can feel my heart beating too fast in my chest, and I wonder if my entire body is flushed with embarrassment.

This is why I avoid people. I'm awkward.

Finally, he shrugs and breaks the silence.

"I think we should start baking. What do you say?"

I nod, not trusting my voice.

"Alright, then, Tink. Let's go."

grady

· · ·

THE KITCHEN IS COVERED in flour and red food dye. I'm pretty sure my fingers will be stained for a week after this.

"You know, I've never been a sweets person," she says, swiping her finger through the leftover icing. I watch as she takes it in her mouth, her pink lips wrapping around it as she sucks it off.

Fuck. Me.

"But this shit is good."

I'm glad that I'm standing on the other side of the island because my dick is threatening to come to life, and that's the last thing I need after I've made so much progress with her.

"And it only took…" I look over at the oven and finally take notice of the time. "Four hours. Shit. We need to get you home. Let's hope the roads aren't covered in ice yet."

She takes one more swipe of icing before grabbing her scarf from the living room. But when I make it over there and get a glimpse of what it looks like outside, I know there's no way I'm getting her home tonight.

"Bad news, Tink." I tug my phone out of my back pocket and check the local online group. Just as I suspected, the roads are impassable. The cops are asking everyone to stay home unless absolutely necessary. And a lot of the county roads around us are already closed.

She looks up at me, her eyes worried.

"What?"

"Looks like you're stuck here." I turn my phone to face her so that she can see I'm not lying. "Roads are closing, and the ones that aren't closed are definitely going to be impassable."

"What?" Her eyebrows tug together as she takes my phone from my hand. I watch as she scrolls through the comments. "No. You have to take me home."

"It's okay, Tink. I have a spare bedroom. You can sleep here."

"No." The grumpy girl I got to know so well over the past year comes back full force. I can see her closing off, her walls building back up one brick at a time. "I am not going to stay overnight here. You need to take me home."

She hands my phone back to me and then crosses her arms, like it's going to make a difference if she takes a stand. It's not. There's no way anyone except the road crews could make it. I glance out the window, and the sleet continues to rain down, freezing everything instantly.

"You have a truck."

"I do," I concede. "But that doesn't mean it's safe."

"I live like fifteen minutes away!" I can see the panic in her eyes, like a trapped baby bird.

"Kara." I take hold of her shoulders gently and make her look at me. "I cannot take you home. I'm really sorry, but it's just not happening. I refuse to risk both of our safety, okay? I have a spare bedroom. I will give you something to sleep in, and if you just really don't trust me, the door has a lock on it."

Her face changes and drops.

"I'm sorry. I didn't mean —" She sighs. "I didn't mean for you to take it like that. I trust you, of course I do. You may not be my favorite person in the world," she says with a laugh, "but I wouldn't ever think you'd do something. I'm just, I don't know. I'm new here, and it's a small town. Everyone is going to know I stayed here. People will talk."

"Who cares?" I give her a squeeze that I hope she takes as a comforting gesture. "You're literally stuck here. You have no choice. And it's late," I finish as she holds back a yawn.

"I am exhausted. This whole thing," she says as she gestures between us and all around the kitchen. "This whole thing has me stressed."

"Come on, let me show you the room."

I walk her upstairs and show her around, letting her know again that there is a lock on the door if she wants to use it. I wouldn't blame her if she did. The bathroom is attached to her room, so there's no need to come out into the hall at night, which I think settles her mind a bit. And when I hand her one of my shirts and pajama pants I know will be too big for her, she gives me a grateful look.

"I'm sure the pants will just fall off, but the shirt should be big enough you could wear it as a nightgown." I laugh awkwardly.

"I appreciate this." Her eyes are red-rimmed, probably because it's after eleven.

"I'm sorry. I should've paid closer attention to the time. I should've made sure we were leaving before it got bad."

"I could've as well." Her shoulders lift in an exhausted-looking shrug. "It's fine. I'm sorry I overreacted."

I'm not sure what to say next, and our words hang in the air. Hank is already in his bed in my room, ready to go to sleep for the night. We're alone with nothing but the sound of the sleet hitting the window. Her dark eyes are hooded, and her tongue darts out slowly to lick her lips. I wonder if she knows what she's doing to me. Is she teasing me? Tempting me?

I can't help but hope that maybe there's something there on her part. Maybe we've both been fighting this, and that's why she's always run in the other direction.

"Um, good night?"

Definitely not something there for her. She's just waiting awkwardly for me to leave, and I'm just standing here like a fucking idiot, waiting for something to happen. Christ, I must be delusional.

"Sorry. Yes. Good night. Just come get me or text me if you need anything, okay? And make yourself at home. *Mi casa es tu casa.*"

I back out of the room like I'm afraid she's going to

make a run for it or something. She just watches me the entire time, her teeth digging into that plump bottom lip while she fights a smile. At least she finds me funny and not annoying.

"Good night, Grady. Thanks again."

grady

. . .

HER BEDROOM DOOR clicks shut behind me, and I all but sprint back downstairs to try and clean up a bit before bed. I take a gummy, my nightly routine to help me sleep, and get to work closing down the kitchen. I don't know why I'm not just leaving this for the morning. That's what I would normally do. But I don't want her to wake up to a messy house and think less of me. Christ, everything I do lately is to impress that girl upstairs.

I hear Hank on the stairs, coming down to check on me. He's probably wondering why the fuck I didn't come to bed. It is way past that dog's bedtime. So as he lies next to the oven, soaking up the heat that's still coming off it, I turn on the soft lighting and turn off the overhead lights to make it a bit more comfortable for him.

As I clean, my mind strays back to her, to what she might look like in my T-shirt, naked underneath as she climbs into bed, the sheets running over the soft skin of her legs. I wonder if she'll fall right asleep or if she'll lie there awake, maybe thinking about me — about what she said earlier.

I know it embarrassed her, and I should've laughed it off immediately, joking to put her at ease. But this dance we're doing, where we act like we can barely stand each other, is getting exhausting. There was a part of me that wanted to come right out with it.

Like, yes! Yes, you beautiful, frustrating woman! I think I'm in love with you!

I finish loading the dishwasher and start it. The sound of the water drowns out the rest of the house creaks and groans that come with remodeling a century-old home. Sometimes being alone in here freaks me out at night. I don't believe in ghosts, but no one can tell me they don't get scared when random noises start up when it's dark outside.

"Grady?"

Her voice makes me damn near jump out of my skin.

"Christ, woman!" I grab my chest and breathe heavily as I try to calm down.

She laughs, and it goes straight to my cock. Especially when I finally really look at her. Because not only is she in my house at midnight, but she's wearing nothing but my T-shirt. Her nipples are hard and tenting the soft fabric. She's decided not to wear the pajama bottoms I gave her, which gives me a nice view of her creamy thighs.

Her eyebrow cocks as I groan, my gaze directed only at her body. I'm self-aware. I know that I'm staring. But I can't stop it. The most beautiful woman I've ever seen is standing half-naked in my kitchen, and all I can think about is throwing her up on the island and having my way with her.

"I was just coming down for some water." Her voice is quiet but heavy, raspy with whatever she's feeling from my intense stare.

I nod, mumbling something about how she can help herself. But I'm still watching her. My eyes flit from her face to her chest to her legs and bare feet, her toes painted a dark brown.

"Stop staring at me like that."

Her tone is almost begging, but I've lost all control. The comforting feel of the gummy has kicked in, letting my guard down and hindering my critical-thinking skills. She takes a step — just one. I look back up to her face only to really like what I see. Because she's not looking at me like she wants me to stop. She's looking at me like she wants me to do something.

Another step in my direction.

"Kara." My tone is a warning, begging her not to come any closer. I don't trust myself. I want her too badly. I've wanted her too badly for an entire fucking year. And now we're alone, stuck in this house together all night, and my mind is running wild with the possibilities.

Another step. Her delicate fingers touch the cool stone of the island and drag as she takes a few more steps toward me until she's so close I'm drowning in the warm, fiery scent of her.

"Can I tell you something?"

Her dark eyes are laser focused on my own, like she's

trying to read my mind. Now she's so close our torsos bump together. Her back is against the island, and one of my hands cages her in while the other remains on my hip, giving her an out if she wants it. It's taking every ounce of my willpower to not lean in and kiss those flushed cheeks before tasting those full, red-velvet-stained lips.

I just nod.

"When I first moved here, I was determined to hate you."

That has my attention.

"I didn't like you much," she continues. "You stole my table."

"Actually, you stole my table."

"Toe-may-toe, toe-mah-toe." She shrugs and grins as her hands reach out tentatively to loop her fingers through my belt loops. If I wasn't hard before, I am now. My dick is straining painfully behind my zipper, waiting for her hands to stray a little further down…

"But after that, something happened." Her cheeks flush even darker. "I had a dream."

Oh, fuck me.

"I'm sure you can guess what kind of dream it was." Her voice is small now, barely above a whisper, as I watch her intently. "And I moved here for a fresh start. I was determined to hate you, because if I hated you, I wouldn't be tempted by you."

My other arm moves to the counter, caging her in on both sides. I lean forward and down to her level. There's a good foot between us, so it's a bit awkward at first, but I need her to look at me.

We're inches apart, our eyes locked together. I can feel her breath skirt across my lips, and I can't help but glance down just as she wets them.

"Why didn't you want to be tempted by me, Tink?"

"I was supposed to be starting over." Her head drops back slightly so that she can look at me more easily. "You weren't in the cards."

"And I am now?" I can hear the gravel in my own voice, the need I feel for her leaking out. Her pupils are blown in the dim light, and I hope it's because she feels what I'm feeling. "Answer me, Kara. What do you want from me?"

"Don't make me say it," she whispers.

"What do you want, baby girl? Something to take the edge off?" My hands slide from the counter to her hips. "You want to take advantage of being stuck together for the night?"

I tug her flush with my body, showing her just how badly I want her as well. I'm trying to show her that she isn't the only one feeling this way. She gasps as I force her body to grind against my own, giving my cock a small amount of relief from the pressure.

"Grady."

Oh, god. I'm a goner. The way she says my name has my fucking toes curling. I abandon her hips for her throat, wrapping my hands around the sides until my fingers tangle in her hair. It's short, but there's still plenty to pull as I expose her neck to my mouth. There's no turning back now. She's given me an opening, and I'm too weak of a man not to take it.

kara

. . .

"Is this what you came down here for?" He lightly kisses the sensitive spot below my ear. My pulse jumps against his lips.

Yes. I groan inwardly. *Yes, this is exactly what I wanted.*

I don't know what came over me. I really did come downstairs to get a glass of water. But then I noticed he didn't hear me come down, and Hank was asleep at his feet, waiting patiently for his dad to finish up. And something deep in my brain went a little crazy as I watched him clean the kitchen, humming to himself as he did.

The look in his eyes when he saw me standing there, naked underneath the thin T-shirt he gave me to sleep in. I know my nipples were hard from the cold and were giving him a nice little show. He absolutely ate me up with his eyes, making every little bit of resolve I thought I had just crumble away.

"Kara." He groans, his breath hot against my ear. It

sends shivers down my spine and a throbbing deep in my belly. "Tell me to stop."

Laughable. Absolutely laughable that he thinks I could stop him now.

Instead, I reach up, grabbing his face, and pull him down to meet my mouth with his own. We clash together, our lips instantly moving and opening for each other. He tastes like the sweet cream cheese icing, and I eagerly swipe my tongue against his.

His cock is hard beneath his jeans, rubbing hard against my stomach as we hold each other, a tangled mess of impatient limbs and greedy mouths. He growls, and I sigh, melting into him. This has to be the best kiss I've ever had. Grady knows what he's doing with every stroke of his tongue, and it makes my thighs clench, thinking about what he could do elsewhere.

"Do you know how badly I've wanted this?" he asks as he pulls away.

Those green eyes of his are even more intimidating close-up. He looks deep into my eyes, trying to convey something I'm not sure I'm ready to accept. Because I'm thinking this could be a quick thing, something that happens once and then we never speak about it again. Just something to take the edge off, like he said. I just... need him right now.

"How badly?"

My fingers play with the hem of his shirt, pushing it up and out of the way. I want to feel him. I get it up to his chest, and he tugs it off the rest of the way, throwing it to the side. Hank gets up and leaves, thankfully not wanting to stick around for the show.

"Wow." I exhale and look over his strong body. The curve of his stomach and hardness of his chest. His biceps are huge and his forearms dusted with blond hair. I can't get over how much he looks like a *man*. Everything about him makes my blood run hot.

"I know." His voice has turned quiet and shy. "Baker's belly." He tries to laugh it off, but I know insecurity when I see it. I am very well acquainted with it.

"I love it," I tell him, running my palms over the length of his torso before grabbing his hand. "See?"

Guiding his hand up my thigh and under the borrowed shirt, I let his fingers find where I need them most. Another growl escapes him as he feels just how wet I am. All for him. Christ, I'm soaked. And as his fingers circle and tease, my knees get weak.

"All this for me?" he asks, dipping a single finger inside before rolling up and over my clit. He does this over and over again, teasing me with just enough pressure and speed to get me to the edge.

"Grady," I whisper, my hands clutching his arm for support. "Fuck."

Just as I'm about to lose my goddamn mind, he stops. My pussy clenches, and I whimper at the loss of him. I was so close. But before I can complain, he grabs my hips and lifts me up onto the island. Watching his strong hands rub and dig into my thighs is so fucking hot. They massage almost to the point of pain, but it just makes my need grow higher.

And then he's helping me lie back, his hand cradling my head while the other holds my lower back. My feet automatically go to the edge of the counter, and he pushes the shirt up and over my breasts. His mouth captures one, his tongue flicking and teeth biting. My back arches off the cool granite as pleasure sweeps through my body.

Mielle was right — this is what I needed.

"You're beautiful," he murmurs against my heated flesh as he kisses his way down my stomach, pausing to kiss and lick every soft spot he comes across. "So fucking beautiful, Kara."

He kisses the dip at my hips and then kneels between my legs. It puts his face right above the counter height, and I know I'm blushing while he spreads my legs further apart.

"Wow," he whispers on an exhale. "I knew she'd be pretty."

"Oh, fuck." I groan and cover my face with my hands. "That is simultaneously the hottest and most embarrassing thing anyone has ever said to me."

"Hush." He licks straight up my center, making my hips jump violently off the counter. He encircles my hips with his arms, pinning me flat against both his face and the island. I can't move as he licks me again and again.

"Oh, god, Grady." I grab a fistful of hair and try to tug him closer. I'm losing my mind, grinding and rotating against his mouth like I need it to survive.

"That's it, Kara, baby." He sucks my clit into his mouth. "Show me what you like."

"Everything." A pitiful laugh escapes me. "Everything

you're doing. More. I want more. Please."

I can feel the vibration against my clit as he laughs and murmurs. I'm lost, though. I can't see or hear. The orgasm is building, the heat flooding my muscles with pleasure that I can't fight. It builds and builds until everything snaps. I cry out, my thighs squeezing his head and my fingers pulling his hair. My breathing stops as I hit the peak, and then I fall back into my body, delirious and boneless.

He continues to lick and suck, nibbling softly on my lips before kissing my thighs. His mouth is wet from my release, leaving goosebumps in his wake in the cool air. My stomach heaves with the effort to get my breathing back to normal. I don't think I've ever felt like that, even when playing with myself.

"That was—"

"Mind-blowing?" he asks, standing up with a very proud look on his face, his glasses tilted slightly off-kilter.

"Cocky much?"

I put my foot on his chest and give him a playful shove. But he just grabs it and deflects by sinking his entire body between my legs. The way he is so tall and is able to cover my body with his makes me feel incredibly safe. My brain shuts off when he kisses me again, the taste of myself on his lips. I tug him closer by wrapping my legs around his waist and digging my heels into his ass.

"Fuck, Kara." He kisses me everywhere. My lips, my cheeks, my eyes, my hair. "You are perfect, do you know that? So fucking perfect for me." His hips grind into mine, highlighting just how true his words are. "I won't take it any further if you don't want to," he says against my throat. "It was enough for me just to touch you, let alone taste you. We can stop. Just say the word, Kara. Tell me to stop."

My heart almost explodes out of my chest. His hands and mouth move over and against my body like he's worshipping it, like he can't ever get enough of it. He moves against me like he loves me. I can feel the panic setting in. This was just supposed to be something fun, something to take the edge off. I'm not supposed to be here, getting attached. This place was starting over, moving on.

"Wait," I all but choke out, the emotions flooding my brain. It takes him a second to register what I've said, and by the time he does, I'm rolling out of his grasp and landing on the cold wood floor.

"I'm sorry," he says, holding his hands up in front of his chest like he's afraid I'm about to bolt out into the night. "No more. I promise."

"I just — I can't, Grady. Shit."

And before he can say anything else, I bolt upstairs. This time, I use the lock.

grady

· · ·

THERE'S a few inches of snow outside, and judging by the way Hank is slip-sliding around, I'd guess there's a thick sheet of ice on top of it. His paws aren't even breaking through as he sniffs out the perfect spot to do his business. The coffee machine stops whirring, signaling it's done, and I forego my normal milk and sugar because I honestly figure I'm going to need the strength of drinking it black.

There's a woman upstairs who is about to be very, very angry that she's stuck in this house with me for another day...at least. I called my buddy who works down at the Department of Transportation, and he's saying even the main highways are bad. Living down South, we aren't really prepared for this type of weather, especially when it comes out of nowhere. And not only that, but it's supposed to snow again this afternoon, meaning the weather really wants her to stay.

I'm standing at the sliding glass door, watching Hank

carefully try to make his way back inside, when I hear footsteps coming down the stairs. My stomach flips and flops, anxiety churning up my gut. What happened last night was stupid of me. I should've never taken it that far. But she slid my hand up under that shirt, and fuck, she had me on my knees — literally.

"Good morning," she says, her voice full of false bravado. It makes me smile. I should've guessed she's come down here with a battle face on.

"Good morning," I answer, opening the door for Hank. "Want some coffee?"

I finally turn to face her, and her beauty damn near takes my breath away. She doesn't have any of her stuff here, so she's barefaced with damp, wavy hair. The T-shirt I gave her last night is still hanging loosely from her body, but unlike last night, she has the pants on this morning. They dwarf her.

"Please."

Her feet are glued to the hardwood, like she's terrified to get any closer. I hate that there's something weird between us now. A really big part of me wants to close the gap between us and sweep her off her feet, kissing her until that attitude of hers crumbles. Well, most of it anyway. She can keep the snarky remarks because I love a woman with a fire in her belly.

"Want to talk about last night?" I look at her over my shoulder as I get her coffee going. I have a single brew, so we have a minute of downtime before it's ready. May as well use that time to grill her.

"Judging by the way your driveway looks, I'm

guessing I'm stuck here. So we may as well." She sighs and climbs up onto a barstool. It swivels as she kicks against the island.

"My knee-jerk reaction is to brush it off." I lean back against the counter so that I can see her expression as I talk. "I'm really good at sweeping things under the rug, ignoring them until they become a giant elephant in the room. But I don't want to do that here, okay?"

"I shouldn't have let it go that far." Her eyes struggle to meet mine, but I can tell she's really trying. I guess knowing you're stuck with someone in an ice storm makes you try a little harder. "Like I told you before, I came here for a fresh start. I was leaving a lot of stuff, including boys, behind."

"I'm not a boy, Tink." I have to say, I'm a little sick of hearing her talk about boys. "I'm a man. I can handle it. You don't have to tiptoe around my feelings. Honest and open communication is what makes relationships — whether they be friendships or otherwise — work. So if we're going to be anything other than enemies" — she smiles at my air quotes — "we need to get past this."

She nods, rolling her lips and biting them nervously.

"Unless you don't want to." The coffee machine stops whirring, so I grab her mug and walk it over to her. I move slowly, knowing she could bolt like a scared rabbit at any second.

"What do you mean?" Her eyes narrow as she brings the coffee to her lips. I watch, remembering with crystal-clear clarity how they feel and what she tastes like. Kara must be able to see it in my eyes because a pink blush sweeps across her freckled cheeks.

"Well, maybe we don't move past it. We move through it." I shrug, taking another step toward her. She's close enough now that I can smell my shampoo on her. I like that she smells like me, like she's mine. "We're stuck here. It's supposed to snow even more. All we have to occupy our time is baking and…"

"And…?" Her left eyebrow cocks up, the understanding sinking in.

"And repeats of last night. But without the whole you running off thing."

She snorts. "That would not be smart."

"Why?"

"Because emotions."

"You think I can't control my emotions?" I scoff, making a show of rolling my eyes. "Please."

I'm lying through my teeth. I can't control my emotions, not when it comes to her. I know I'll fall hard and fucking fast. No brakes. It'll probably end in a horrific, fiery crash. Like the ones you know you shouldn't be watching but can't help to look at. One of those. But the ride would be so worth it. Tasting her again? Feeling her come on my tongue and fingers? Hearing her moan as I hit just the right spot? Christ. Fuck, I want that. I want that more than I want anything.

I jerked off twice last night, the taste and smell of her still on my lips, and it still wasn't enough. When Hank woke me up this morning, I was already hard again, knowing she was just down the hall, her bare legs tucked under the soft covers and hair tousled from sleep.

"It's not that I regret what happened."

"You just hate me and everything about me?" My joke falls flat.

"I don't hate you." She rolls her eyes, the attitude I've come to know and love coming out to play. "You're just endlessly happy. Always smiling. Like, do you ever stop?"

To prove her point, I smile even wider.

"Never."

"That's what I thought. You'd get sick of me and my perpetual rain cloud."

She sees herself as grey clouds and downpours, always grumpy, but I've never seen someone shine so brightly. Everything about her is electric, making you want to see what she makes happen next. She's strong and resilient. I'd love to be able to make her not only see that about herself but believe it.

"Grass can't grow without a little rain."

I wink at her and earn a smile.

"Anywho, just a thought. But you won't get any awkwardness out of me. As far as I'm concerned, we are two consenting adults that had a little fun." I shrug and finally remember I still need to feed Hank. He comes running when he hears the kibble. "I say we make some breakfast, put on a good movie, and figure out what the hell we'll be doing for my part of the competition this weekend."

The sigh that escapes her mouth sounds heavy, like there's so much more she wants to say. But I won't rush it out of her. I'm a patient man when it comes to things I want.

"Alright, then, Captain Cheerful." She takes a deep breath and resets. "Let's win this fucking contest."

"Atta girl."

kara

. . .

H~AVING BEEN BORN~ and raised in ~~Being from~~ the Midwest, this is blowing my mind. I don't understand how the roads can be so bad when it barely even snowed. Sure, it's icy. But can't they just throw some salt down? Grady tells me it's because they're just so unprepared, and it happens so few and far between that they don't really keep snow and icy stuff on hand.

Ridiculous. Because now I'm stuck here all day, and it doesn't look like it's going to be getting better anytime soon. It's snowing again, and it's getting down into the single digits tonight. He's worried about pipes freezing, and I'm worried about maintaining my self-control for another night.

"So, you're telling me that *this* is your favorite Halloween movie? Really?"

We're splayed out on his sectional, blankets and bags of snacks between us, and *Halloween H20* is playing on the

67

TV. We've been taking turns watching our favorite movies, and I just so happen to love scary. First, it was *Paranormal Activity 3* — I love the fan scene; the slow, tortuous rotating of the camera gets me every. damn. time. And now, it's the 1998 Halloween movie with Josh Hartnett and Michelle Williams. It's so bad but so, so good.

"It was the first one I ever watched in this franchise, actually," I tell him, laughing at his expression. "I know, it's the weirdest one to watch first. But I was over at a friend's house, and I didn't want to seem lame for not having seen any of them before." I shrug. "It's taken a special place in my heart."

"The acting is…"

"Phenomenal? Oscar-worthy?"

"Bad," he deadpans.

We both laugh. This has been fun. He's managed to make sure nothing between us feels awkward. It's like we've slipped right back into how we were before the little escapade last night. I would be lying if I said I wasn't thinking about it every time I caught him looking at me or every time we accidentally brush up against each other on the couch. But I appreciate that he's not made it awkward.

"Wait." He sits up straight, his hand flying over to smack my leg.

"Ow, what?" I say over a mouth full of pickle chips.

"I have an idea for the competition." This piques my interest. We've been volleying ideas back and forth all day, trying to figure out something that is sweet and on theme while still having a little Kara flair to it.

"Spit it out!"

"You like horror movies. We should do something horror themed."

"It's Valentine's Day. I don't think horror and Valentine's mix."

"What? Have you lost your mind?" Hank flicks his ears as his dad's raised voice wakes him up. "Of course it does. We need to do one of those heart cakes. I'm seeing them everywhere lately, with the cherries on top and the old-fashioned-looking icing. And then, when you slice into it — preferably with a massive butcher knife or something — red raspberry goo will ooze out like blood. And we can replace the cherries with raspberries to match the inside. Put our own little twist on it."

Okay, I fucking love that idea.

"Yes. Yes. How do we make that happen?"

An hour later, we are in the kitchen, red icing literally everywhere, and Grady is putting the finishing touches on the cake. I didn't help a lot because everything he was doing looked complicated. I basically stirred the batter, and that's it. The cake is beautiful. A bloody red icing covers the entire heart-shaped cake, and then he piped more of the same color in sweeping designs around the sides. On top, he wrote, "Be My Valentine," in a large, cursive font, and then in small letters at the bottom, he wrote, "or else."

"Ready for the pièce de résistance?" he asks as he grabs a very large butcher's knife from the block on the counter. His smile looks a little wild and crazy as he flips it in his hand.

It does something for me. That fun, wild look in his

eyes is giving me butterflies. I like seeing him let go around me. All day, he's been having fun trying to make me laugh instead of pressuring me into picking up where we left off last night. It's a new type of feeling to be around him. It sounds stupid to say, but he makes me feel safe. Like I can be myself around him and he'll still like me at the end of the day. There's no putting on a happy mask just to make him feel comfortable. He likes me, attitude and all.

"Do it." I wag my eyebrows at him, hoping that I'm matching his wild expression with my own.

His arm flies through the air in dramatic fashion, stabbing the cake right in the center. He pushes it through and then stabs it again before slowly pulling the slice out from the cake. Bright red raspberry-flavored goo oozes out onto the countertop. It looks amazing and screams Kara.

There's a weird flood of emotions going through me. We've had fun all day, watching movies and getting high, only to eat our body weight in snacks. Thank god he keeps this place well stocked. He's been himself all day, not giving me any silent treatment because I stopped him last night. There's no anger or resentment. It's been like he's just happy to have me here. And now he's spent the last hour working really hard on making sure this cake is as much like me as it can be.

Our eyes meet, and his smile is broad. His pretty green eyes are all but glowing from excitement behind his glasses. It's infectious. Before I know it, I'm squealing and jumping into his arms. The knife clatters onto the countertop as our lips meet again. It's a quick one, just a peck on the lips. Like it was a natural reaction to cutting a cake.

I pull back, and we look at each other. He's shocked. His eyes are wide, and the corners of his mouth are tugged up in a surprised smile. His arms are wrapped around my body, holding my feet off the ground and my body flush against his. God, he feels good. I could get used to being wrapped up in these strong arms. And with that thought, I decide to let go a little. Will I regret it tomorrow morning? Who knows. I hope not. Because this feels too right to ignore.

I bite my lip for a second, grab his face with my hands, and then pull him in for another kiss. His soft lips meet my own, and we are off to the fucking races.

kara

. . .

GRADY WASTES no time in taking control of the situation. His hands move down my curves to grab hold of my ass, his fingers digging almost painfully before they sweep lower to my thighs. I get the hint and wrap my legs around his waist. The baggy pajama pants of his that I'm wearing make it a bit difficult, but we make it work. I don't think anything could stop me from seeing this through this time.

I barely recognize that we're moving until he drops me softly down onto the couch. It's snowing, and the sun is setting. The fire is roaring across from us, the shadows making him look even more impressive than he is. His shirt comes off, showing off the broad expanse of his chest and the soft curve of his stomach. He lets me get my fill of him as I run my palms over the hair on his chest.

"Fuck, you're hot."

My voice is rough and full of wonder as I look him

over. I've never been with anyone like Grady. He's author-itative without being overbearing. He's kind and gentle but isn't afraid to poke fun and test my boundaries. And if last night is anything to go off, he's very, very good in bed.

"Your turn," he says with a smirk. I hold my arms above my head and smile up at him.

Grady takes his time, making sure I feel his fingers move my shirt away from every inch of my skin. It tickles, causing gooseflesh to erupt over my stomach and arms. My nipples harden at the sensation, and he growls when they finally come into view, exposed and ready for him. My shirt is barely over my head before he's ducking down to capture one hard nub in his mouth.

"Grady!" I cry out, clutching hard onto his head to keep him right where he is. His tongue flicks over my nipple before he nips at it with his teeth. Reluctantly, he moves to the other, giving it the same treatment.

My panties would be soaked — if I were wearing any.

"Do you know how hot it is to hear you say my name like that?" His gruff voice is muffled against my skin. He moves over me like he can't bear to be torn away, his mouth, teeth, and tongue tasting every inch of me until he gets back to my mouth.

"Tell me we're doing this." It almost sounds like a plea, like he's begging me, and that really gets me going.

As an answer, I kiss him hard, biting his lower lip until he groans and thrusts his hips against my core. I'm hot and needy, and fuck, he feels huge. His cock is rock hard beneath his sweatpants, and once he starts, he can't stop.

The pressure on my clit feels fantastic, and heat begins to build deep in my belly.

We break apart from each other just enough for me to work my pants past my hips. He helps me lift my ass off the couch to get them down the rest of the way, and before he can move, I shove his sweatpants down roughly with my feet. His boxer briefs are the only thing between me and that massive cock of his. And even they're barely able to contain him.

"Wow, Grady," I say in a bit of awe as I run my fingertips over his length. He shudders and closes his eyes as he takes a deep breath. I smirk up at him when he opens his eyes again. They look wild and frantic. "That's impressive."

"An entire year." His voice is gruff as his thumbs dip under his waistband. "An entire year of watching you and wanting you." The briefs get pushed down, exposing the delicious length of him.

"Christ," I say, my voice barely above a whisper.

"I never thought I'd have you, Tink." Once his boxers are completely off, he grabs me under my knees and spreads my thighs wide for him. I'm completely on display and feeling more than a little self-conscious. I can't even tell you the last time I shaved.

I swore off men, remember?

But Grady is looking at me like he wants to eat me alive, and I'd be lying if I said I didn't want exactly that.

"So you'll forgive me when I can't hold back?" His green eyes finally look up to meet my own. They're wild and wide, his pupils nearly eclipsing the irises.

"I wouldn't dream of it."

"Good." He fists his cock and strokes it base to tip, once, twice, and then notches the head at my center. "Because I need this, Kara. Need you."

He thrusts forward, so slowly it's torture. The stretch is intense, but he soothes me as he sinks inside, whispering sweet nothings against my throat until he's fully seated inside. My pussy clenches against him, causing a strangled gasp to escape his throat.

"You feel perfect, my sweet storm cloud." His teeth nibble at the hollow of my throat. "You are perfect. Am I hurting you?"

I take a deep breath, my mind and body trying to process everything at once. My emotions are all over the place. The way he touches me and speaks to me makes my heart beat painfully. The way he's notched so deeply inside of me makes my thighs and my breath tremble. Fuck, I'm surrounded by him. Every part of him touches every part of me, and I wasn't expecting it to be this overwhelming.

"No," I finally manage to say. "No, I'm okay." I smile up at him before he descends on my mouth again, claiming it just the way he claimed the rest of my body.

"You say stop at any time, and I stop immediately." He kisses my forehead, and then his hips begin to move as he pulls back. "Okay?"

I nod because I can't speak right now. I feel everything too much. I'm overwhelmed by him.

"Please use your words, Kara." He kisses the corner of my mouth. "I need to hear you."

"Yes, I promise. Just, please, Grady." I'm whining now,

practically begging him to fuck me. I just need him to fucking move. "Fuck me."

That's all he needed to hear. With my permission, his hips slam back into me. The sloppy, wet sounds of us mix with the crackling of the fire. I lift my hips to match each thrust, flexing my abs and trying to get him to go as deep as he can. My nails dig into his back, urging him on.

"My god, Kara." He kisses me again and again. "Perfection."

I push on his chest, shoving him back on the couch as I swing myself up and over his lap.

"I like you like this," I say with a grin. "Underneath me and at my mercy."

He smirks like he's about to say something smart, but before he can, I grab hold of him and sink back down, relishing the way he fills me so perfectly. His mouth drops open, and his eyes roll back. One hand goes to my hips, urging me to grind against him, and his other hand lies flat against my belly so that his thumb can tease my clit.

"That's it, baby girl." His gruff voice urges me on as my hips roll against him. My arms rest on his shoulders, and my hands tangle in his soft hair. There's a need deep inside of me, burning me up and taking control.

"I can't wait to watch you come all over my cock." His voice barely registers I'm so far gone. "Use me, Tink. Come for me. Let me see how pretty you look coming all over my thick cock. Tell me how good it feels."

"Oh, fuck!" I cry out. I can't help it — his dirty words are doing all sorts of crazy things to me. "You feel so good. Too good. I'm so close, Grady. I'm so close."

I'm panting now as his hips make little thrusts underneath me, hitting a deep, throbbing spot inside of me. Over and over again, the thick head of him brushes against that sweet spot, making my entire body light up.

"That's it." His thumb picks up the pace, matching the rest of our frantic movements. "You're so close, aren't you, sweetheart?"

"Yes." I barely get it out. My eyes are closed, and my body is moving on its own. I'm lost in the pleasure of it all, barely able to even register I'm still on planet fucking Earth.

"Look at me, Tink. Look at me when you come. I want you to know who made you feel this fucking good." The last few words are ground out through his teeth.

I obey instantly, my eyes flying open only to find his staring right back at me. Whatever I see in them sends me over the edge. My mouth drops open as I choke out his name, my entire body going stiff as pleasure sweeps through me.

"I'm going to come, Kara. Tell me where. Tell me where you want me." He's panting, my hips still moving beneath me. His features are pained as his pleasure mounts.

"Right here," I tell him, leaning forward and grabbing his mouth with my own. "Don't you dare pull out and leave me empty and wanting."

"Fuck!" He comes with a roar, my mouth catching most of it as I kiss and nibble his lips. His abs flex and tremble underneath me, his cock twitching as his cum spills deep inside of me.

grady

. . .

SHE COLLAPSES AGAINST ME, our bodies slick with sweat. I'm still in the aftershocks of the most intense orgasm I've ever experienced. The world is tilting, and I'm struggling to stay upright.

"Wow," she breathes against my ear as her arms wrap tighter around my shoulders. She fits so perfectly around me, and I fit so perfectly inside of her. It feels like it was meant to be, if you believe in that type of thing.

"Wow, indeed," I say, my voice still shaking. I huff out a laugh. "Shit, I think you broke me."

"I broke you?" She laughs and pulls back to look at me. "I think it's the other way around, Lurch. My pussy has been utterly ruined for anyone else."

"Thank god for that," I murmur, kissing her swollen lips. "Now I don't ever have to share you."

I realize what I said right after the words escape my mouth. It's not that I don't mean them — I do. I never ever want to share her. I want her to be mine. I mean, shit, I've wanted this woman since I first saw her a year ago. It's not like I'm moving at lightning speed. I've had a year to come to terms with how I feel about her. And even though she's always kept me at a distance, I knew I'd fallen hard for her.

What can I say? I like a woman that can put me in my place. Verbal sparring is my foreplay.

But Kara just laughs, letting her head fall down to rest on my shoulder.

"I would like to formally apologize for the rushed job," I tell her, cringing when I realize we jumped right into the act. No foreplay whatsoever. But when I had felt just how wet and eager she was, my dick overrode all logical thought. "I promise I know how to restrain myself and be patient. I should've given you so much more."

"Nothing to apologize for." She leaves a sweet kiss on my neck. "Trust me. I wanted it just as badly as you did."

"Worried you'd talk yourself out of it?" I tease.

"Partially," she admits. "It's easy for me to get inside my own head."

I stroke the soft waves of her hair and pull her tighter against me. I want her to know it's okay, that I don't judge her for it. I want to tell her all about how I care for her and how I want to take care of her. There's so much I've held back on for the past year that it threatens to spill out of me.

But I'm terrified of scaring her off. I have a history of falling too quickly, and the last thing I want to do is fuck this up. And then it finally registers that we just had sex... without a condom.

"Fuck, Kara." I push her back so that I can look at her. "I just came inside of you."

"Mhm." She nods eagerly, her pretty dark eyes practically glowing. "I was there."

"Birth control?"

"Yes, Grady." Her laughter is raspy and sweet. "I would've stopped you otherwise."

"I should've stopped myself," I groan, laying my head back on the couch. "You make me lose my mind a little. I should've taken my time, teased you, and played with you a bit. I'm off my game."

She laughs again, and fuck if it doesn't fill me with so much happiness to hear.

"I'm clean, by the way. Bit late to say now, I guess. But I never would've gone forward if I wasn't. I got tested after my last relationship and haven't been with anyone since."

"Same," she admits. "But since we're here now, I guess I can admit that I have a little *thing* when it comes to having sex without condoms."

"What now?" I perk up and look at her. That gets my attention.

"Don't judge me." Her cheeks are bright red.

I make the sign for Scout's Honor.

"I just like the way it feels. The whole coming inside of me without a condom thing. I think I have a bit of a breeding kink but without the breeding."

If my cock wasn't ready for round two before, it

certainly is now. Holy fuck. This woman was made for me, a gift wrapped in a dark bow. Her head sinks down to rest on my collarbone, effectively hiding her face from my view.

"Well, that's fucking hot," I tell her honestly.

"Is this going to be weird now?" I swear I can hear the embarrassment in her question.

"Not as long as we communicate," I tell her honestly. "Tell me what you want, Kara."

She moves, the shifting of her body teasing my dick all over again. Christ, he's almost ready for round two already. This woman is going to be the absolute end of me. I hold her face gently in both of my hands, letting my thumbs caress her cheeks as she looks at me with a softness I'm not used to from her.

"What do you want, Tink?"

She grins.

"To win the competition."

I roll my eyes.

"We can start there." I kiss her softly, and I love the way she just melts into me. Her chest sinks against my own, and her hands explore my body. "But eventually," I continue, "we'll have to talk about it."

She hums against my mouth as her nails rake across my nipples. That little jolt of pain goes straight to my dick, waking him up fully as she starts to move those delectable hips of hers in little circles.

"Think you have another in you?" she asks, her eyes opening to catch me staring at her.

"Do you?" I wink at her playfully. "Because I've been

rock hard and ready to go ever since that little kink comment a second ago."

I give her ass a smack.

"And if we're sharing," I continue, "then I should probably tell you that I am very, very fond of marking you as mine. Whether that be by coming inside of you or leaving you covered in handprints and bite marks."

Her pussy clenches tightly around me at my confession, and I bite back the groan of pleasure it causes me. Fuck, she is so tight and wet. I'm desperate to move inside of her again.

"Do you like that idea, sweetheart?" I smack her ass again, feeling her skin warm beneath my palm. She clenches again. "Like that I want to mark you up as mine?"

"Fuck," she says on an exhale. Her pupils are blown wide as she looks at me with so much lust I think I'm going to explode right here and now, not caring just how embarrassing that might be. "Yes."

"Good girl." I knead and dig at the flesh of her ass. "Now, I'm going to take you upstairs, tie you to my bed, and show you just how patient of a man I can be."

kara

. . .

HE STANDS up in one swift motion, taking me with him as I squeal out of shock. He's still lodged deep inside of me, and I fucking love it. I don't know how or when it started, but, fuck, I love the idea of him filling me up and keeping it inside of me. I've never been one to want children, but I do really, really enjoy the act of making them.

Walking into the kitchen first, he grabs the leftover raspberry syrup we used for the inside of the cake. I've never done any type of food play before, but if it's going where I think it's going — him licking it off every sensitive part of my body — I am totally down for it.

"Hold this, Tink." I grab it from him with a grin before putting a little on my finger and sucking it off so, so slowly. His gaze heats as he watches my lips wrap around my finger and suck off with a pop.

"Tease," he growls.

I just laugh and give him a kiss, letting him taste the

sweetness of the raspberries on my tongue. His hands dig into my ass, spreading me as we make our way upstairs. His fingers crawl to my center to tease me. Just the tips play along the crack of my ass before dipping lower to massage me around where his cock stretches me wide. I'm panting as the slight pressure makes everything feel so much more intense. And when another finger slips backward, teasing the place where no man has ever been, I can't help but moan against his throat.

"Has anyone ever been here, Tink?" he asks as we reach the top of the stairs. My nails are digging into his shoulder blades as every part of my body tingles and warms under his touch.

"No," I manage to squeak out.

He pushes through just enough that I feel the burn. I try to relax, taking deep breaths. It's an odd mixture of emotions, fear and pleasure. Everything feels heightened and sharp.

"Good. It's mine." He bites down on my shoulder hard enough to leave a mark, but I love it. I love feeling this normally so reserved and sweet man kind of losing it because of me.

We finally reach his bedroom, and he tosses me down on the mattress like I weigh absolutely nothing. I bounce once, twice, and then scoot back to the headboard as his cock stands proudly between us. I can feel both of our releases leaking out of me, but I'm too eager to see what he's going to do next to care.

"Here," he says, holding out his hand as he rounds the corner. I hand him the bottle of syrup and then watch him pull a few lengths of rope out of his nightstand. Next comes a bottle of lube and then a blindfold. My pussy is clenching in anticipation.

"Who knew Lurch was such a freak in the sheets?" I ask, a teasing tone to my voice.

He just returns my joke with a panty-melting grin. How in the hell did I end up here? I was so determined not to get involved, but this damn ice storm had other ideas. I guess I just decided to take that as a sign. I'm not one to read horoscopes or believe in crystals — well, not completely, anyway — but I will take something as a sign if it's slapping me across the face.

"Lay back, sweetheart."

Something in my chest thaws at the sweet little nickname, and I do as I'm told, eager to get this show on the road. The rope is black and soft with a little stretch in it as he wraps both of my wrists together and then ties them to a spot on the headboard. It's a metal loop that has been screwed into the thick wood. Damn, this man takes his kinks seriously.

I love it.

Next, he ties my ankles separately to each corner of the mattress with loops that seem to sit underneath the mattress. I'm spread wide open for him, and he looks me over appreciatively, like he's very proud of his handiwork. His cock bobs as he walks around the bed, the tip leaking precum that I'm very eager to get a taste of.

"My eyes are up here, Tink."

I smirk and pull my eyes away from the monster between his thighs.

"But your cock is so much nicer to look at."

"Oh, you are so going to pay for that."

"Oh, I sure do hope so."

He picks up the squeeze bottle of red raspberry syrup and begins to drizzle it over my body. I watch as the liquid makes spirals across my chest and stomach. Grady crawls in between my thighs, tossing the blindfold next to my head on the pillow before leaning over my body and licking one long line from my belly button to my right nipple. He sucks it into his mouth and rolls his tongue over my nipple again and again until all of the syrup has been sucked off.

He does this over and over again, all over my chest, stomach, and hips. I'm writhing beneath him, my hips raising to seek out any friction they can find. But each time, he pulls away, just out of reach.

"Grady!" I groan and tug against the ropes, desperate to be able to touch him and urge him on. The answering chuckle that comes from him is deep and fucking annoying because I know he's enjoying this. He says he loves my attitude, well, he's about to make it flare back to life.

"Can I help you with something, Tink?"

"Touch me!" I beg him. "I can't stand it any longer. Please."

"Look at you," he all but purrs as he sits the syrup to the side and crawls up my body. His cock sits heavily on my thigh. "You look so pretty when you're all flustered and needy. Beg for me again, sweetheart. Let me know you really mean it."

"Grady!" I growl out.

He looks at me expectantly, the head of his cock barely nudging against my core. He reaches for the blindfold while he waits and slips it gently over my head to black out my vision completely.

"You tell me if it gets to be too much," he whispers close to my ear. "Say the word, and I stop. It can be a lot when your vision is taken from you. Heightens everything else."

I swallow nervously.

"Now, beg, Tink."

I'm too turned on to defy him. I'm needy and dripping. My clit is throbbing in time with my heartbeat. I am fucking desperate for him. I can't handle this teasing any longer.

"Please, Grady," I beg him, my voice merely a whimper. "Please, touch me. Let me come. Do whatever you want to me, just please fucking touch me."

"Okay, sweetheart," he says. "No need to get upset."

He laughs, and I growl.

"Not. Funny."

And then his mouth is on me. My hips jerk into the air at the sudden sensation. He takes my clit into his mouth and sucks so hard I think I'm transported to a different plane of existence. Holy shit, this man knows what he's doing. He works me into a frenzy, not giving me a single break as he eats me like a starving man, our mixed releases from earlier coating his tongue when he dips inside.

The orgasm comes hard and fast, lighting me up from the inside out. I scream, my wrists tugging hard on the ropes. I hear the metal clamps on the headboard creak as I tug and tug, my muscles seizing up. My thighs are tight around Grady's face, and I wonder if he's even able to breathe down there at the moment. But my pleasure trumps any sort of anxiety I might have at the moment.

My toes curl, my heartbeat speeds up, and my breath catches. All the while, Grady is still sucking and licking. He adds a finger and then another, letting them curl deep inside until he finds the little button that causes me to fucking detonate.

I cry out again, and this time, the pleasure is white hot and blinding, one orgasm flowing swiftly into two. My muscles contract and then release, and I can feel myself squirting all over his face. Grady hums and moans as he continues to lick me through it.

"Fuck me, Kara. You are a gorgeous sight to behold, do you know that?" He licks me right up the center one more time. "And you're all mine, aren't you?"

"Yes." The word hisses through my teeth as he teases me.

"Good. Very good girl."

I feel the mattress dip as he moves around. His knees are on either side of me as he continues to move up my body. I know where this is going, and I get a thrill when I feel the tip of his dick resting against my lips.

"Can you open for me, sweetheart?"

grady

. . .

SHE OPENS up those plump lips for me, giving me silent permission to slip inside. My balls tighten with pleasure as the slick warmth of her tongue caresses the underside of my shaft. I sink in until I feel the back of her throat. She relaxes, letting me move even farther down her throat. No gag reflex. Fuck me. I'm so far gone for this woman.

Without her eyes or hands to guide her, she's just at my mercy. I fuck her face slowly and gently, not wanting her to get overstimulated or worried that I'm pushing her too hard. Plus, I like taking my time with her. I'm enjoying this far too much to rush.

"That's it," I praise her. "You're doing so well for me, Kara. Taking me so well."

That elicits a moan, and the vibration goes straight through my cock, making it weep with need. Fuck, I need to be inside of her now. I slip out of her mouth reluctantly, and the cutest pout forms across her swollen lips.

"I was having fun."

"Yes, well," I say, tugging the blindfold from her face. "You're about to have more of it. Just bear with me, Tink."

Her mouth opens for me as I kiss her, savoring the taste of our releases mingling together. She gives me the sweetest little sighs and moans as she tries to grind her body against my own. But I tied her tight enough that there's no way she's getting free. She can tug as hard as she wants; she's not going anywhere.

Running my hands over her soft skin, I sink back down her body to untie her ankles. I rub them to make sure she isn't in any pain. She never told me to stop, but I just want to take care of her. I've wanted to for so long now.

"Letting me go?" she asks, a teasing tone lilting in her voice.

"Not a chance, sweetheart."

I flip her over and grab hold of her hips, lifting them so that I have the most perfect view of her ass. My thumbs press into the soft flesh there, prying her open. Her sweet, pink pussy is swollen and dripping. As I take my time drinking in the beautiful sight, her body clenches in anticipation.

"Think this pretty pussy can handle some more?" I use the tip of my finger to tease her tight opening.

"I can handle whatever you throw at me, Lurch." She turns her head to the side, looking back at me over her shoulder. "You seem to be running out of steam, though. Need a break?"

Her lips are tugged into a smirk. She's teasing me, pushing me. Cheeky little storm cloud. I smack her ass hard enough to leave a handprint. I watch as red finger-prints appear on her creamy skin. She moans and shakes her ass at me.

"Thank you, sir. May I have another?" She bites her lip, and my cock twitches. Fuck me.

I slap her again, this time on her other cheek, leaving another blooming handprint. Her breath is coming in hard and fast. I know her ass is burning, and I don't want to push her too far. I'm worried she won't tell me to stop because she's too damn proud. So instead, I lean forward, reaching past her to the nightstand, where I sat the lube. I pour some over her crack, watching it drip down against her heated lips. She sighs in pleasure when the cool liquid runs over her clit.

"Ready for round two, Tink?" I toss the lube to the side and begin to work a single digit into her ass. It's tight, so fucking tight. Groaning, I push it into the first knuckle. She squeezes the absolute life out of it. "Don't worry, sweet-ness. I won't be fucking you here today."

I swear I feel the tension leave her body as my finger slides into the second knuckle. My cock is weeping, ready to go again, so I notch at her entrance, spreading the lube around her sensitive flesh. I don't want her to be so sore she can't sit tomorrow, but I would like her to be sore enough to remember what happened here.

"Just fuck me already!" She groans in frustration. "I can't handle this teasing!"

She pushes back on me, causing both my cock and my finger to slide farther inside of her. We both sigh as our bodies come together again. She feels perfect, so fucking perfect for me. I lose myself in her. I run my free hand up her spine and grab hold of her hair, tugging it back.

Kara's little noises are music to my ears, and when she begins to really move her hips, fucking me as I fuck her, it's like I'm transported out of my body. The pleasure is unreal, seeing her like this for me. She's facing away from me as I tug on her hair, her spine curved, and her ass pushing high up into the air for me.

"So fucking beautiful," I tell her over and over again. "Next time I fuck you, we're doing it in front of a mirror. You have to see what I see. So perfect."

"Grady." My name escapes her mouth in a moan.

"That's right, baby. Are you going to come for me?"

"Yes," she hisses. "Right there. Please don't stop."

I keep the pace, chasing my own orgasm as hers builds. My balls are heavy and ready to explode as they clap against her clit with each thrust. Our bodies smack together, the wet sounds filling the room. I just know my bed will smell like her after this. I can't wait.

Within seconds, her sweet pussy is pulsing around my cock as she screams so loud her voice disappears into a whisper. I don't even try to hold back — I come right along with her, the heat exploding up my spine as her juicy little cunt works me for all I'm worth.

Spent, I collapse on top of her, my cock slipping free as I roll to my side. I immediately untie her wrists, letting her hands drop back to the bed. Kara's eyes are closed, her breathing deep and measured as I rub her wrists. Finally, after a long minute, her dark eyes open and zero in on me.

The sweetest smile tugs at her lips. She looks positively sated.

"Who would've known?" she asks, running her left hand over my ribs and around to my back. I tug her closer.

"Hmm?"

"You fuck just as good as you bake, Lurch."

I throw my head back in laughter.

"You're not so bad yourself, Tink."

We lie there for a moment, our breathing the only sound in the room. I could get used to this, holding her tightly against my body as she drifts in and out of sleep. I glance over my shoulder to look out the window. The snow is still coming down, and the sun has almost completely set now. Hank will be needing his dinner, and Kara will be needing some aftercare.

"Hey, baby." I gently push the stray hair out of her face. "Let's get you cleaned up."

She groans, and her lower lip sticks out in a pout.

"I know," I say with a quiet laugh. "But I think a shower will make you feel so much better. And then I could whip us up something for dinner. After I make sure you're fed, you can sleep as long as you want."

Those pretty eyes open, and she takes me in for a moment. I can feel myself freeze under her gaze. Does she like what she sees? I would be lying if I said I was terrified that this was a onetime thing. I'd respect her decision, but I wouldn't be happy about it. I don't want her to ever leave my bed. Every time I get in it, I want to smell her on my pillow and all over my sheets. I want her here. I want her to be mine.

"Okay." A soft smile makes my chest ache.

"Okay." I kiss her, gently scoop her off the bed, and carry her to the shower.

kara

. . .

THE SUNLIGHT BREAKS through the curtains, and Hank is at the side of the bed, nudging my hand with his nose. I scoot over closer to Grady, and his arm immediately snakes around my stomach, holding me tightly against his warm body. After patting on the bed next to me a couple of times, Hank jumps up and snuggles up.

"You smell like Fritos," I tell him, kissing his large snoot. "You pull a double shift last night at the factory?"

Grady huffs a laugh behind me.

"He works nights." His nose runs up the back of my neck before I feel his lips leave a trail of kisses. "And so do we recently."

That earns a laugh out of me. We've been going at it like rabbits the past couple of nights, only coming up for food and the occasional shower. After I kissed him that day, I stopped letting my anxieties get in the way. Grady feels good. He treats me well, feeds me like he's taken me to raise, and washes my hair when we shower together. If you've never had your partner wash your hair for you, I highly suggest you give it a try. It's so relaxing and feels intensely romantic.

"Roads will be open today," he murmurs against my shoulder. "I should take you home."

That throws a bucket of cold water all over our cute little bubble. I knew it would come back — the real world. I wasn't sure what that would mean for us. Mielle has always said that Grady had a crush on me, and clearly, that was true. But how far does that crush go? And not only that, but how far does my own little crush go?

Is this going to become more? Are we going to go public with this? Because this town is so small that the rumors are probably already spreading. Mielle knows I'm here because she checked in on me once the roads closed, and I know she wouldn't tell anyone. But Agatha knows I'm here as well, and that woman's mouth runs so fast she could win the gold in the Olympics.

"You are thinking so hard there is smoke coming out of your ears, sweetheart." He kisses me again, his lips soft against the side of my throat.

"Sorry." I roll over to face him, throwing a leg over his thigh. "Just thinking about what this looks like outside of the storm."

I can barely look at him, worried that the rejection is coming. He's older than me. He has his life together. And I'm just a fresh-out-of-college girl with almost forty thousand in student debt and a credit score that is less than optimal. On top of that, I'm an asshole. I've been a dick to the poor guy for a year, throwing snide remarks in his face any chance I got while also talking shit behind his back to Mielle until I was blue in the face.

"What do you want it to look like, Kara?" His voice is soft, kind. Always so kind to me. When I don't answer, he pushes on. "Because I want it to continue. I'd like to hold your hand when we walk down the street and kiss you when I bring you a danish in the mornings."

"You never bring me danishes," I tease him.

"Yeah, but now that I know they're your favorite, I'll bring one to you every morning." He smiles and kisses my nose. "I'll bring you anything you want, Kara. I'll do anything you want. I'll *be* anything you want. Just say the word."

"I sound like a broken record," I tell him, sighing. "My ex… I think he did some permanent brain damage. I just got so tied up in making sure this move was for me. It was to start over and focus on myself and what I liked to do. No one telling me otherwise. No one holding me back."

"Is that what you think I'd do?" he asks, her eyebrows scrunching together. "Do you think I would hold you back or tell you what you can and can't do?"

"Never," I say, my voice sure and firm. "I know you wouldn't. And I think that's what's thrown me for such a loop. I think there was a part of me that assumed any relationship meant I couldn't be myself."

"That's not a relationship, Kara." His voice is so gentle, and his fingertips tuck my hair behind my ear before tracing patterns down my arm. "I promise that if you want to see where this goes, I will support you no matter what.

I'll lift you up. I'll make it happen. I'll be your go-to guy for anything and everything. I want to be that for you. I want to see you succeed."

The tears threaten to fall over. My throat feels like it's closing up. After hearing my ex go on and on about how stupid and pointless my ideas and dreams were, this means the world to me. And I don't even think Grady knows just how much I needed to hear it from him.

"My sweet little storm cloud." He grabs my face and pulls me in for the sweetest kiss. "I just want to hold your hand."

I laugh, wiping away the few stray tears that made it out.

"I guess we can start there."

"I also want to win."

That really gets a laugh out of me, and Hank gets annoyed by the noise, huffing as he jumps off the bed.

"I think we're going to win," I tell him.

Hank barks from where he sits at the bedroom door. His tail is wagging, and I'm sure his stomach is growling. I look at Grady and feel an overwhelming amount of peace with this decision. Mielle is going to flip.

"We should feed him," I tell Grady. "And then we should go into town and make sure both of our places are intact. After the horror stories you told me about pipes bursting, I'm a little more than nervous about my poor little coffee shop."

"Alright, then. The woman gets what the woman wants!" He stands and throws on a pair of boxers that hug his ass oh so perfectly. God, this man has a great body.

"Your clean clothes are sitting on the drawers in the closet. I'll make breakfast." He kisses me one more time and then gets Hank riled up. "Let's eat, Hank!"

I sit up on my elbows and watch them both dance and jump around each other before Grady opens the door and Hank shoots out like a rocket. Grady looks back over his shoulder, giving me a wink, and then follows his sweet boy down the stairs. I fall back onto the bed and breathe in his scent. For the first time in a really long time, the butterflies in my stomach come to life, and I can't stop the smile that grows so big it hurts my cheeks.

Storm cloud, meet sunshine.

kara

. . .

"I NEED TO VENT," Mielle announces as she walks into the coffee shop. Her normal smiling demeanor is replaced with a scowl. I've never really seen her upset, so this is new.

"Sit," I tell her, gesturing to our favorite little window nook. The shop is closed today for the street fair, and I've just been prepping all morning. "What's up?"

She groans and sits crisscross applesauce, hanging her head in her hands. I reach out and run my hands over her forearms. It's sunny today, the snow has melted, and the high is in the sixties. It's a wild turnaround from the ice storm we had a few days ago, but welcome to the South, I guess.

I'm not complaining, though. Normally, I don't like warm, sunny weather. I've always been a fan of rainy days. They're cozy and comfy. But something about the sun coming out after Grady and I finally got over ourselves and came together — literally — is a welcome sight.

I look across the road to his Pepto-pink bakery and smile when I see him putting the finishing touches on our cake. He looks so concentrated, like this is the most important thing to get right. He knows how badly I want to win this contest today, and he's really taken this all so seriously to make sure we get our trophy.

"I just ran into someone." She looks up at me through her fingers. I quickly direct my focus back to her. "Remember that little story I told you before you started banging Grady? About how the best sex of my life was with someone I hated?"

I laugh at her little comment about me banging Grady and nod.

"He's back."

"Who's he?"

"Reid." She rolls her eyes with dramatic flair. "Reid Lyons. Je le déteste."

Okay, I'm not even that into sports, and I know that name.

"The football player?"

"Of course you know who he is," she almost growls. "His ego would love that."

"Okay, so you ran into him. That doesn't mean—"

"He's back." She cuts me off and pouts, crossing her arms over her chest. I don't think I've ever seen Mielle so worked up before. "I guess he got injured in the last playoff game. He lost, by the way," she says with glee. "But it's a career-ending injury, I guess."

"God, that's awful. How's he doing? That has to be hard."

She gives me a look that could freeze over Hell. I hold up my hands and lean back. I don't need to get on Mielle's bad side. That's the last place I want to be. That woman can make a grown man cower in fear if she gets angry enough. I wonder if Reid Lyons has ever shrunk or if he stands up to her, and that's why she hates him so much.

"I don't care about his career. I care that he's back in town. For good." She sighs. "Kara, run away with me."

"What?" I laugh out loud. "I already ran away once, Mielle. Remember? That's how I ended up here."

"Merde." Her head goes back to her hands, and I can tell this has really upset her. She takes a deep breath, and when she exhales, her breath is shaky.

"Mielle, mon amour. Tell me what's wrong." I reach out and grab her hands, forcing her to look at me. "Tell me."

She looks at me, her blue eyes bouncing back and forth between my own. I watch as she takes a deep breath, blinks away the tears, and then flips the switch.

"Non," she says. "Ce n'est rien. Nothing that you should be worrying about. Especially not today."

A fake smile is plastered across her face, and I go to say something, to insist that she confide in me. I'm her best friend, and she's mine. After all she's helped me through this past year, I consider her like a sister, and I want to be there for her. Competition be damned.

"Mielle—"

"How's it going with Grady?" She wags her eyebrows and nods in his direction. I decide to let it go for now. If she doesn't want to talk about it now, that's fine. I can always grill her later when she's ready.

"Fine," I say with a sigh. "Better than fine, actually. He's kind of…" I fight to find the right words for just how amazing that man is.

"Perfect for you?" she asks, an eyebrow cocked up towards her hairline. "Just like I said he probably would be?"

I roll my eyes and nudge her with my knee.

"I get it. I get it. I should've listened to you and Agatha." I shrug. "Guess we just needed to be shoved together forcefully and locked up in an ice storm for me to get over myself."

"That's all it took?" she asks, a real smile playing on her lips. "Wish I'd have known that earlier. I would've made that happen so much sooner."

"Ah, yes. Because you do control the weather."

"Exactly."

We both laugh and settle into silence while we watch people begin to set up their tables outside. The entirety of Main Street is taken up by big white tents and tables that will soon be filled with delicious Valentine's Day treats. Grady walks out of his bakery with a huge cake box and grins when he sees us both sitting in the window seat. God, it lights up his entire face.

"Gross. You are looking at him with puppy dog eyes," Mielle teases. "Sickeningly happy."

"Good morning, ladies," Grady says as he walks in, coming straight to me to kiss my absolute socks off. "I missed you last night."

"I'm sitting right here," Mielle says as I stare up at my handsome man.

"I missed you as well, Mielle. I haven't seen you in far too long." He kisses her cheek and then sits our competition-winning cake on the counter gently. "Want me to help you start carrying your machinery out?"

"That would be amazing," I tell him, joining him behind the counter to start carrying out what I need. It's not too much; this stuff is just bulky and awkward as hell to carry.

"I wish I could join the winter festivities," Mielle says as she joins us. "My bees would kick your cake's ass."

"You don't even know what the cake looks like," I tell her, narrowing my eyes playfully at her. Grady and I decided to keep it a secret until it's time to unveil it and stab it violently so that everyone can enjoy it together. Mielle is dying to know.

"You two bicker like an old married couple sometimes," Grady comments as he picks up the espresso machine. "Should I be jealous?"

Mielle kisses me hard on the cheek, I'm sure leaving a red imprint of her lips behind.

"Always," she tells him with a grin. "Now, tell me how to help."

grady

. . .

MY GIRL IS NERVOUS. Her whole leg is shaking as we wait for the judges to approach our table. They do this every time, wait to judge the person who won last year. I don't really mind it because winning these competitions doesn't mean as much to me as it does to Kara. But this year, I'm just as nervous as she is. I want her to get this win.

"God, what is taking so long?" She's whispering, but she may as well have yelled it.

"We're next, Tink." I kiss the side of her head. "We've got this."

As Agatha and the rest of the judges appear, we both stand and present our creations. The cake gets unveiled, and Kara puts the finishing touches on her coffee. I have to admit, they look good together. We added a bit more coloring to her coffee to make it match the dark red icing of the cake, and she had the brilliant idea of adding edible glitter to the entire cake. It makes it shimmer and sparkle in an incredible way.

When she comes back and slides the coffee across the table, she notices that I changed the wording on it. It takes her a second, but finally, she sees it.

"Will I be your Valentine?" she asks, looking at me with those big, brown eyes. Damn, I get lost in those pretty orbs so easily.

"Will you?" I ask, feeling Agatha staring at us so hard she might light a fire. "Will you be my Valentine, Kara?"

A smile breaks out across her face, just like when we first came up with this idea, and before I know it, she's jumping into my arms all over again. I grab her, pulling her close and kissing her hard. I don't care who's watching. Everyone needs to know this woman is mine.

"Of course I will be," she murmurs against my lips. "Of course. Of Course."

We get lost with each other, the competition forgotten as our mouths move against each other.

Until Agatha clears her throat.

"I, for one, am absolutely thrilled that my plan worked."

"You control the weather now, Ags?" I ask her, letting Kara slide down my body and back to her feet. I don't let go of her, though. I want to hold her against me a little while longer.

"I put you two together for this!" she exclaims, her smile big and bright. "I could've put you with other people, let you continue your little feud."

"Yes, Agatha. I'm sure they're both ecstatic that you took such an interest in their love lives," Mielle chimes in.

"Here!" Kara hands Agatha the first coffee and then hands out four more to the judges, who have been watching this all with interest. I'm guessing Agatha told them why she did the new setup for this Valentine's Day, so I'm sure they're all eager to see how we did together.

"And now, for the cake," I say, grabbing a huge knife from under the table. I went to the store yesterday to find the biggest knife I could. I wanted it to be dramatic and really spray the fake blood all over the cake and the plate beneath it.

"Now, that's a knife," Mielle says, trying her best at an Australian accent.

Kara snorts.

"Here we go!" I pull my arm back like I'm recreating the scene from *Psycho*, ready to stab violently into the deep red cake. I hit it with force, the blood bubbling up and covering the top of the cake and knife. I pull out and stab again. I do this a few times to really get the blood-spatter effect before cutting the first piece.

Everyone is clapping and talking to each other. It's a hit. And when I look down at Kara, she's smiling from ear to ear, with a little bit of stray raspberry syrup dotting her cheeks.

"Got a little on you," I say, swiping the red drops from her cheek with a finger and popping it in my mouth. Her eyes heat immediately, and I know it's taking her right back to that night we spent in my bed, her body covered in the stuff as I licked it off.

"This is delicious, you two!" Agatha cheers, completely missing the fact that Kara and I are having a moment.

"Amazing, really," another judge says. "How did you come up with the idea? It's so unique!"

"This girl loves horror movies. We got stuck together in the ice storm," I explain. "And when we were watching her favorites, it just came to me. The coffee was all her, though."

"It's honestly the best pairing we've seen," Agatha mock whispers. "I wouldn't be surprised if you take it home again, Grady."

"This time, it'll go in her shop," I say, nodding in Kara's direction. "She's got the perfect spot for the little trophy on her shelves behind the bar."

"That's so sweet," Agatha croons.

They talk amongst themselves for a while longer while everyone else has a piece of cake until we are completely out. Kara has run out of ingredients for her coffees, and every last bit of cake has been eaten. And when it's time to announce the winners of this year's contest, I hold Kara in my arms, her back to my front, while they give the speech.

I can feel her body humming with energy and excitement. We sway back and forth slowly, Mielle standing at our side. They're holding hands, and I love seeing how supportive they are of each other. Honestly, without Mielle, I don't think Kara and I would've stood a chance. Kara told me all about how Mielle has been in my corner throughout the year, teasing Kara about how much I liked her. I'm grateful that they have each other. They both deserve a friendship like that.

"And the winner of this year's Valentine's Day competition is…!" They pause for dramatic flair, and Kara's body goes rigid. Her free hand is wrapped around my forearm, and her anxiety is causing her short nails to dig into my skin.

"Kara and Grady from Roasted and Temptations Bakery!"

The crowd cheers and claps, and Mielle screams as she tugs Kara in for a hug. It's quick, and soon, she's shoving Kara in my direction. I take the hint and scoop her up, kissing her hard on the mouth.

"We did it!" she cheers when she pulls away.

"We did it, Tink." I grin at her and then kiss her again, barely able to control myself. I can't wait to take her home and celebrate in private.

She jumps out of my arms and runs across the street to jump up onto the makeshift platform they've made for announcements. The little heart-shaped trophy is placed in her hands, and she bows in dramatic fashion as everyone claps. She looks beautiful. Her hair is shining in the February sun, and her cheeks are pink from the excitement.

Fuck, I think I'm in love with this woman.

"You should tell her," Mielle says, nudging me with her hip.

"Tell her what?" I peel my eyes away from Kara just long enough to glance down at Mielle.

"That you love her."

"Did I say that out loud?" My eyes go wide as I look

around. The last thing I want to happen is for someone to overhear that and tell her before I have the chance.

Mielle laughs. "No, but I could hear your thoughts bouncing around."

"We won!" Kara shouts as she runs back into my arms, holding the trophy high.

"No storm clouds today," I say loud enough so only she can hear.

"Nah," she says, shrugging her shoulders. Her eyes are saying all the things. "Sunshine drove them away."

epilogue

. . .

Kara

VALENTINE'S DAY

"Did I ever thank you for everything you did for that competition?" I ask him as I roll up on my elbow. We're lying on a pile of blankets in front of the fire. Hank is sound asleep in his bed, and I am dying for Grady to take off my damn clothes. I wore the sexiest red lingerie I own, and I'm ready for him to see it.

"Hmm," he hums as my hand runs down his chest and over his stomach. "I don't think you did."

"I didn't think so either." I unbuckle his jeans and slide my hand underneath the waistband of his boxers. He's already hard and ready for me as I stroke him from root to tip. The sweetest-sounding groan escapes his throat.

I throw the blanket off his body and make quick work of his jeans and boxers. His cock lies hard against his stomach, precum dripping from the tip. My mouth waters as I strip in front of him. I don't make it quick, though. I want to tease him, make him wait for it.

His eyes stay glued to me the entire time, sweeping across every inch of flesh that becomes exposed to him like a heated touch. God, I swear I can feel it.

"You look fucking breathtaking," he whispers, barely loud enough for me to hear. But I'm finally standing in front of him in just my lacy panties and bra that hug all my curves perfectly. I feel beautiful in this, and with him looking at me like that, I have the confidence to keep going.

I drop to my knees and rake my nails down his thighs before dipping my head. My lips part, and I look up at him as I swallow him down into my throat, moaning as I do. One free hand cups his balls and plays until he is swearing and fisting my hair. I love it when he loses control like this. And I especially like knowing I'm the one that does it.

"Wait, sweetheart," he says as he pulls me off with a pop. "I had plans tonight, and they don't include coming in the first five minutes."

I laugh and crawl up his body, letting his cock slip between my folds. I grind against him, trapping his cock between me and his stomach. The friction against my clit feels amazing, and it doesn't take long before he's soaked and I'm close. So, so close.

"God, you look so beautiful, Kara. Riding me like that. Fuck, so good." He grunts as he lifts me by the hips. "Put me in, baby."

I do as he says, grabbing his cock and lining him up with my entrance. I'm ready and needy, and he slips in easily. He fills and stretches me to my limit, and it feels so fucking good. He's touching every sweet nerve inside of me, lighting me on fire.

Grady sits up, grabbing my ass to help me grind, and then his fingers stray to my ass. He's obsessed, playing and teasing with me every time we're together. I'm hoping tonight's the night. I'm eager to try it out. And I know he'll take care of me. I trust him.

"Grady," I whimper against his mouth. "I want to try it."

"Yeah?" His eyes meet mine, searching to make sure I'm really okay with it.

"Please."

"I want you to come first." He kisses me, and our tongues fight for dominance. When he pulls back, he grins, and his thumb finds my clit. Circling it hard and fast, he pushes me into an orgasm in record time. My eyes roll back, and my thighs squeeze against him. I can barely catch my breath before he's shifting and lifting me up off the ground.

"Good girl." He gives me a firm spank as we make our way upstairs. "Remember, you say stop at any point, and I will stop. I want this to feel good for you, as well. Okay?"

I nod, biting my lip.

"Just breathe," he instructs as he tosses me down on the bed. "And stay relaxed. At any point it's too much, you tell me. You're not allowed to be too proud and push through the pain. Got it?"

I nod again.

"Words, please, Kara."

"Yes, I agree." I smile up at him while he digs the lube out of the drawer.

"Flip over."

I do as he says and arch my back to give him the perfect view of my ass. He tugs off his shirt and then climbs onto the bed between my legs. The mattress dips as he settles, and then the cool trickle of the lube makes me jump. My clit is throbbing with need as he works it between my cheeks, sinking one finger in and then another.

He takes it slow, checking in with me each step of the way. Each time he pushes farther, he uses his thumb to tease my clit. It distracts my body from the burning stretch as he adds yet another finger. I feel impossibly full, and as I adjust, I reach around and ask him to stop.

"Don't take them out. Just…wait." My voice is breathless, and his free hand rubs up and down my spine with his thumb continues to tease. It takes my body a second to adjust, but then it does, and I relax. I take a deep breath, and with that, he sinks in even more.

"My god, sweet girl." His voice is deep and gravelly, filled with lust that makes my toes curl. "You are doing so fucking well. I think you're ready for me. What do you think, Kara?"

I moan and nod, my body taking on a mind of its own as I push back against him. It feels…good. Really good. And I want more. I want to know what it feels like to have all of him inside of me.

"I'll go slow," he tells me as I watch him put an ungodly amount of lube on both me and him. It's making a mess of the sheets beneath us. "But I know you're going to take me so well."

He's back between my legs, and I feel the firm head of him push against my hole. I take another deep breath and relax. It takes a second, but he pushes through, causing an intense burn to sweep through my body.

"Okay, wow. You are a lot bigger than your fingers."

He chuckles softly, his hand snaking around my hips to ease the pain. As he plays, the burn subsides, and pleasure replaces it.

"Keep going," I beg him.

"Fuck," he grinds out, another inch stretching me wide. "You're so tight, Kara. This is going to be embarrassing for me."

I can't help but laugh at that.

After a few more minutes of slow progress, he's fully in, and I am panting with the need to come. Every time his artful fingers stroke me close to the edge, he pulls back, teasing me endlessly.

"Grady, stop teasing me."

"I like teasing you, though." He slowly pulls out and then thrusts back in. There's no more burn, just sharp, all-encompassing pleasure. "How's it feel, baby?"

A moan is my only response as his hips thrust out and in again. Who knew this pleasure could be this intense? His fingers tease in time with his thrusts, and before long, my orgasm is right there. My head drops to the mattress, and my stomach clenches. I cry out his name as I come over and over again.

"Fuck, baby. That's right. Come while I fuck this tight

little ass of yours." He smacks me hard, the pain only adding to the pleasure that's thrumming through my muscles.

"Come for me, Grady." I urge him on, thrusting back to meet his hips. I can feel that he's close, his movements becoming erratic as he gets closer.

"Fuck! Kara!" I feel him empty inside of me as his dick twitches and his body stills. He falls forward, and his breath skates across my back.

Slowly, he pulls out, making sure not to hurt me in the process.

"Oh, fuck," he says again, collapsing to my side and pulling me tightly to his body. We are both sweaty and spent...and ready for a shower. "You were perfect."

"What a cliché," I tease. "Getting anal on Valentine's Day."

He laughs and kisses me sweetly.

"Kara." His voice is quiet as he strokes my hair out of my face. "I think I'm falling in love with you."

I can't hold back the smile that forms. Sure, it's fast. We've been sleeping together for just over a week, but we've known each other for so much longer. We've had a year of foreplay. A year of getting to know one another whether we were meaning to or not. We may not have been doing this part for very long, but he knows me. And I know him.

"And you don't have to say it back. I don't want you to say anything until you mean it. But I wanted you to know."

"I'm falling for you, too, Grady," I tell him honestly. "I'm sorry my spitefulness kept us apart for so long."

His soft lips find my own, and I melt into him. When we pull back, he smiles and winks.

"All you needed was a little sugar."

want more sweetwater?

Mielle's story coming soon...

also by dana isaly

about the author

Dana Isaly is a Romance author that has dipped her toes in dark, paranormal, and even romcom.

She was born in the Midwest, grew up in the South, went to university in England, and even spent a couple years in California. She is a lover of books, coffee, and rainy days.

She swears too much, loves dogs more than people, and believes that love is love is love.

You can find her on Instagram (@author.danaisaly), join her Facebook group (Dana's Tribe of Horny Humans), or follow her on TikTok (@author.disaly).

Made in United States
Troutdale, OR
02/19/2024

17799735R00083